A Groom for Violet

The Blizzard Brides Series

Laura Ashwood

Anchored Soul Publishing

A Groom for Violet

by Laura Ashwood

Scriptures quoted from the King James Holy Bible.

Cover Design by EDH Graphics
Editing by Carolyn Leggo and Amy Petrowich

God, you brought me to it and you brought me through it. I give all my glory to you.

Rod, I adore you. You make every day a good day.

A man's heart deviseth his way: but the Lord directeth his steps.
~ Proverbs 16:9

Contents

♥

Get Free Books!

♥

Join Lauren's newsletter to get an exclusive novella, stay updated with new releases, recipes and more! You can sign up on her website at www.lauraashwood.com.

Chapter One

♥

March 1879

Heaving a sigh of frustration, Violet Stapleton scanned the mercantile for Phyllis Talley one last time before stepping up to the counter where Mr. Talley was busy refilling a large glass container of colorful penny candy.

"Good morning, Mrs. Stapleton," he looked up and the corners of his mouth lifted from under his thick, dark moustache into a toothy grin.

Violet's brows dipped and she glanced over her shoulder, half expecting to see her mother-in-law, Cora, behind her. Heat rose up her face and settled into her cheeks as she realized the man was speaking to her.

She didn't think she'd ever get used to being called Mrs. Stapleton, even though it had been over six months since she had come to Last Chance to marry Wyatt Stapleton.

They'd been married just a week when Wyatt left with most of the town's menfolk on a hunting trip and never returned, victims of a freak early season blizzard. Violet shook off the errant thought and fixed her attention on the man on the other side of the counter.

She watched Mr. Talley place a small silver scoop in the jar, then turn and set it on the shelf behind him next to several other jars filled with various confections. "Your order arrived yesterday," he placed a lid on the jar, then turned back toward her and reached under the counter to retrieve a small paper-wrapped parcel which he set in front of her.

Violet returned his smile and let out a small sigh of relief. "Just in time. Is Mrs. Talley in? I didn't see her."

Mr. Talley shook his head. "She's visiting Mrs. Purcell. I'm not sure when she'll be back," he shrugged. "Is there anything else I can get you?"

Violet's shoulders dropped a bit. She'd been looking forward to going through the Montgomery Ward catalog with Phyllis.

"Yes, I would also like a small bag of white sugar, please." As she waited for Mr. Talley to measure and weigh the sugar, her gaze drifted back to the candy jars.

A wave of nostalgia came over her at the sight of the jar filled with cherry drops. She could almost see her father standing in front of her as a small child, patting the pockets of his frock coat, encouraging her to guess which one contained a treat. She somehow managed to pick the correct pocket every time, and he'd reach in and pull out a lemon or cherry drop for her. Then she'd wrap her arms around him, inhaling the slightly sweet, earthy scent of pipe tobacco that always lingered on his clothes.

"That'll be nineteen cents" Mr. Talley's voice brought her back to the present, and Violet swallowed back the lump that had formed in her throat. She plucked two dimes out of her reticule and handed them to Mr. Talley, and gave another quick glance to the jars of candy. "Can I also get a penny's worth of lemon drops, please?" She smiled, satisfied with her choice.

While she waited for him to get the candy, Violet reached back into her reticule and pulled out a calling card. It still read Violet Montgomery, but she hadn't had a chance to order replacements yet, and it looked like it would have to wait again. She knew Mr. Talley was capable of assisting her, but Violet felt more comfortable ordering such items from Phyllis.

She was still trying to adjust to life in the small town of Last Chance, and hoped Mrs. Talley might be able to help. Last Chance was so different than Charleston, in nearly every way. She folded the upper right corner of the card over, as was custom, and placed it on the counter in front of her.

The bells over the door chimed and Otis Ignatius Graham stumbled into the store. He staggered to the counter next to where Violet waited and leaned on it with both arms. His brown hair was mussed and his clothes were stained and dusty. The sour scent of body odor mixed with alcohol and tobacco filled the space, and Violet hoped Mr. Talley would hurry.

Otis turned to her, one rheumy blue eye focused on her while the other looked off into the distance, and nodded in greeting. Violet gave the man a polite smile in return and slipped her gloves back on her hands. She let out a sigh of relief as Mr. Talley handed her her purchases.

"Thank you, can you please see that Mrs. Talley gets my..." Violet's words turned into a gasp as she watched Otis pick up her calling card and stick it between his teeth in an attempt to fish out some sort of food particle with it. Violet took a step backwards and opened her mouth, but was unable to say anything.

"I'll be sure to let Mrs. Talley know you inquired of her," Mr. Talley said through gritted teeth. "Give my best to the elder Mrs. Stapleton."

Violet's eyes flitted from him to Otis, who was still picking at his teeth with her card. She blinked several times, then slowly nodded her head. "Th-thank you," she managed, forcing a smile, then turned and hurried out of the store.

She made two quick stops. One at the post office to check the mail for Cora, and the other at the bank, before she climbed into the buggy. Settling onto the seat, Violet pulled her wrap tighter around her shoulders in an attempt to ward off the chill that was now seeping into her bones. It had been considerably warmer when she left the Stapleton house. Cora had warned her how quickly spring weather could change, and

Violet wished she would have remembered to take the buggy quilt with her.

Squaring her shoulders, she carefully threaded the reins through her fingers like Wyatt had taught her and snapped the reins. She turned the horses onto Scott's Bluff Road and headed west.

Winter in Nebraska was much colder than the winters she'd experienced back home. It seemed as though it was always windy and she'd never experienced anything like the blizzards that killed so many the previous fall. While it was true Charleston did occasionally get blasted by a tropical cyclone, they weren't common like the snow and cold here.

The Stapletons' lived just a few miles west of Last Chance, but the ride home today seemed to take much longer than usual. The wind had loosened the knot in Violet's hair and it whipped violently around her face, while tiny pellets of snow stung like needles. Ice covered the road and forced her to keep the horse moving at a slow trot.

A wall of thick, grey clouds replaced the brilliant blue sky from earlier that morning, and created a dreary backdrop for the pillowy white snow drifts.

By the time she reached the Stapletons' farm and brought the buggy to a stop in front of the large whitewashed barn, Violet's fingers were so cold she could no longer feel the reins in her hands. She had no more than brought the horses to a stop when the barn door opened and Eli Stapleton came rushing out to help her down from the seat of the buggy. Her cold feet were unsteady and she was grateful for the assistance.

"Hi, Violet," his whole face spread into a smile as he took the reins from her hands. "I can take care of the horses for you."

Eli was Wyatt's younger brother who, at the tender age of fourteen - make that fifteen today - considered himself the man of the house since Wyatt's death.

"Thank you, Eli," Violet said, and collected her packages from the floor of the buggy.

"It's no trouble," Eli averted his gaze and focused his attention on the horse beside him. Violet watched as a deep red flush she suspected had nothing to do with the cold crept up the boy's neck and colored his cheeks. She suppressed a chuckle and ran stiff-legged toward the house, eager to get out of the cold.

She stepped inside the modest home and was greeted by the delicious aroma of freshly baked bread, and a small, white barking bundle of fur. Violet pulled off her gloves and stooped to pick up the squirming animal.

"Hi Daisy," she cooed in the dog's ear. "I'm sorry my hands are so cold." She tried to stomp her feet to get the snow off her shoes, but they felt like blocks of wood attached to her legs. She hobbled across the room and stood in front of the fireplace, cuddled the dog against her chest, and closed her eyes, trying to will the heat to warm her faster.

"Violet, you're back," said a soft voice from behind her. Violet opened her eyes and turned to face her mother-in-law. She flashed Cora Stapleton a smile, but her cheeks were still numb and she feared it looked like more of a grimace. She was unable to stop her teeth from chattering long enough to say anything.

"Goodness, you're half frozen," the tall, willowy woman lifted the packages out of Violet's stiff fingers and placed them on the table. She then took one of the chairs nestled under the table, dragged it in front of the fireplace, and motioned for Violet to sit down.

Violet complied, got Daisy settled in her lap and wrapped her arms around herself, her teeth chattered together uncontrollably. She couldn't stop herself from shaking.

Cora slipped the damp wrap from Violet's shoulders and shook her head. "Is this all you had on? Didn't you bring the quilt?" She slid a glance at the wooden box on the floor next to the door where the thick quilt she'd told Violet to bring with her still lay in a neatly folded bundle.

Violet cast her gaze down to her lap. "I f-forgot it," she had trouble getting the words out, her teeth were chattering so hard. Deep down, she knew Cora was simply concerned, but years of her aunt's berating her still played in her head. She couldn't bear the thought she might have done something to disappoint this woman who had done so much for her.

"Well, you can use it now," Cora crossed the room and picked up the quilt, then wrapped it around Violet's shoulders. She pulled a tin cup out of the cupboard, filled it with coffee from the pot on the cook stove, and handed it to Violet.

Violet curled her hands around the warm cup and took a gracious sip of the hot, slightly bitter liquid. Comforting warmth spread through her body, her teeth stopped chattering, the tremors subsided, and she began to relax.

Cora filled a cup for herself, slid another chair close to the fireplace, and settled into it. "Was there any mail today?" she asked.

Violet shook her head and watched the glint of hope in Cora's eyes instantly fade away.

Cora sighed. "Thank you for checking."

A wave of sadness swept over Violet. She wished she knew what Cora was waiting for. If she did, she may be able to help. She chewed her lip, thinking how she might ask without being intrusive. She'd been taught that it wasn't polite to inquire about someone's personal business, but Cora was family. Wasn't that different? Yes, she decided. It was.

"Is there something I might be able to help with?"

Cora hesitated, then let out a deep breath. "Planting season is approaching," she said. "Unless Emmett comes home, Eli is going to have to spend more time in the field. He can't possibly do the planting and all the chores, he's much too young," she wrung her hands in her lap. "He already does so much. I may need your help with some of the barn chores."

Since Violet's arrival at the Stapleton farm, Cora had not been willing to let her do much more than simple household tasks. Of course, it didn't help that she didn't know how to do much more than that. She'd been raised with a series of maids in an environment where ladies were to be waited on, and felt completely inept in this different way of life. She was constantly fearful that at any moment, Cora would ask her to leave. This would give her a chance to prove her worth.

Violet didn't hesitate. "Yes, of course. I would be happy to help. You've done so much for me, it's the least I can do." She had no idea what "barn chores" might consist of, but was willing to help in any way she could.

"Thank you," Cora smiled, relief washing over her features. "Perhaps Emmett will reply soon, there's still time."

Emmett was Wyatt's older brother, but very little had been said about him since her arrival. Violet's knowledge of him consisted of the fact that he made a deposit into Cora's bank account each month, and that he'd been doing so ever since his father's death. Aside from that, she knew nothing about him.

She'd been surprised when he hadn't come home after Wyatt was killed, and even more so knowing that still hadn't returned even after Cora had asked him to. *What kind of son would do that?* She knew all too well that money didn't solve every problem, especially if you were a woman.

Violet's curiosity got the better of her. "Where is Emmett?" she asked.

"He's in Denver," Cora said, but didn't offer any further information.

"You don't speak of him."

Cora gazed at the fireplace with a dull stare, the dancing flames reflected in her eyes, but she remained silent.

"Neither did Wyatt," Violet said in a soft voice. Wyatt told her he had an older brother, but said they didn't speak and made it clear that further conversation about the subject wasn't welcome. There was so much about her husband that Violet didn't know. Didn't get a chance to know.

Cora shifted her gaze to Violet and studied her face. "I just assumed Wyatt had told you," she said, shaking her head. "But it doesn't really surprise me that he didn't."

Violet stroked the soft fur of the sleeping dog in her lap and listened intently.

"Emmett and Wyatt have been rivals ever since they were small children. They were so different, you see? Wyatt was just like his father. He loved the land. He could stand and look out over a field, and it was like it spoke to him in some sort of secret language. Eli is the same way. Nothing makes him happier than being outside, working in the dirt."

"Emmett and William," Cora paused and stared at the steaming cup grasped between her fingers with a faraway look in her eyes. She brought the cup up to her mouth with a small sigh and took a sip. "Emmett and William, on the other hand, always had their noses in a book."

"William?"

Cora's shoulders drooped. "William was four years younger than Wyatt. He was killed in the same accident that took their father."

Violet inhaled sharply and covered her mouth with her hand. Daisy shifted on her lap, gave a huff of annoyance at the sudden movement of her master, and closed her eyes.

"Even though Emmett had left by then, Wyatt blamed him for the accident. Said if he'd been there, it never would have happened."

"Is that true?"

Cora shook her head sadly. "No. It was an accident. If it hadn't been William, it would have been Emmett."

Violet leaned forward, careful this time not to disturb the sleeping dog. "What happened?"

"Ernest was cutting down trees in the hollow down by the creek. There were several big oak trees he wanted to fell, but he needed help. Wyatt was in the field, and Eli was far too young, so he took William with him. I told Ernest to wait until Wyatt could help. William was not good with the horses, and not nearly as strong as Wyatt," she explained. "But he wanted to get them down before the snow came."

Violet's heart ached for the tragedy this woman, this family had endured. She was no stranger to what it was like to lose someone close, but this woman had not only lost her husband, but two of her children. She reached over and grasped Cora's hand, giving it a gentle squeeze. "When did this happen?"

Cora's brows furrowed a moment. "It was five years last fall." She returned the squeeze and placed her other hand on top of their joined hands, then continued. "They were trying to pull a large log up the side of the hill. It had rained the day before and the ground was damp. The horse slipped and the chain snapped," she trailed off, closing her eyes. A tear ran down one cheek and disappeared under the collar of her dress. She cleared her throat and continued.

"The chain hit William in the head, and Ernest didn't have time to get out of the way. By the time we realized something was wrong, Ernest was gone. William hung on for a few hours, but his injury was too severe to overcome."

They sat in silence for several minutes. How awful that must have been for Cora. Violet's thoughts filtered back to her Aunt Dorcas telling her that her parents weren't coming back. A shiver ran down her spine. *No! She was not going to allow herself to think about that day.* She swallowed down the lump in her throat and gave Cora's hand another squeeze. "I'm so sorry," she said.

Cora glanced at the clock on the mantle and jumped to her feet. "Oh my goodness, I didn't realize it was so late. I need to get the cake made."

Daisy, startled by the movement, let out a yip of displeasure and Violet gently placed her on her cushion near the fireplace hearth, where she promptly curled up and went back to sleep.

Violet stood. "Let me help you," she followed Cora to the cabinet and watched as she pulled out a large bowl and placed it on the table. Violet reached for the package of sugar and handed it to her. "I brought some white sugar for the cake," she grinned.

"Violet, you shouldn't spend your money on such frivolous things," Cora half-heartedly chided as she reached for the bag, unable to hide the smile in her voice.

"*Birthday cakes should always be sweetened with white sugar*, is what my m-mother . . ." Violet stumbled over the word, the lump in her throat threatening to return. She swallowed it back down and continued, "always said."

She reached for the package containing the order Mr. Talley had given her and unwrapped it.

Fifteen small, narrow candles lay nestled in the paper. "And they should always have candles."

"Eli has never had such a birthday treat," excitement flashed in Cora's eyes. She quickly measured ingredients into the bowl and made a thick batter.

It never ceased to amaze Violet how mixing together items that would be inedible on their own, could magically turn them into any number of delicious dishes. Their cook back in Charleston was competent, but couldn't hold a candle to Cora Stapleton. Violet wondered if she would ever master the skill. She would inevitably leave out an ingredient, or over or undercook whatever it was she was attempting to make.

Violet watched Cora expertly pour the cake batter into a cast iron skillet and made a mental note to order her one of the special cake baking pans she'd seen her old cook use next time she was at the mercantile.

"I can make whipped cream for on top of the cake," Violet offered. *Surely she couldn't mess that up*.

Cora hesitated just long enough to make Violet wish she hadn't asked. She had ruined a number of dishes since her arrival because of her incompetence. But to her surprise, Cora agreed.

Violet carefully poured the cream into a bowl and added a touch of the white sugar, just as she'd seen Cora do many times before. Then, using a whisk, whipped the cream as fast as she could.

The muscles in her arm were screaming by the time stiff peaks began to form in the bowl, and Violet was determined to make them as high as possible. But instead of getting taller, she watched in horror as they started to shrink. Violet switched arms and whipped harder, but the faster she went, the lower the peaks went and the thicker the cream became. Defeated, she removed the whisk from the bowl and turned to Cora.

"What have I done wrong?" she frowned.

Cora glanced into the bowl and started laughing. "You've made butter."

Chapter Two

♥

April 1879

E mmett Stapleton suppressed a groan as the stagecoach swayed and jostled over the last few muddy miles into town. When he left Last Chance at seventeen to chase his dreams, he never planned on returning to the farm where he'd grown up. When he left the second time, after the funerals of his father and brother, he swore he'd never return. Yet here he was.

Emmett peered through the window as they barreled toward Main Street, and was amazed at how much the small town had changed. It was still little more than a poor farm town compared to Denver. The streets in Denver were lined with businesses on both sides. Countless people and numerous carriages filled the vast roads of the large city. Not like here, where it seemed to Emmett as though every other building was boarded up and empty and the sidewalks were deserted.

The mud splattered stagecoach rolled to a stop in front of the depot. The door opened, pulling Emmett from his thoughts. He waited while the other two passengers, a couple of younger men, disembarked before taking his turn. He'd been forced to endure their incessant prattle for hours about the women they were coming to Last Chance to meet.

Fools, he shook his head. As far as he was concerned, the very idea of arranging marriage through correspondence was preposterous. How could one possibly ascertain compatibility in that manner? Not that he was an expert in those matters himself, he was far too busy with his career aspirations to be concerned about courtship. His mentor in Denver, John Hanna, the man that had taken him, as a naive green farm boy, under his wings and turned him into a gentleman, wasn't married. It wasn't necessary as far as he was concerned.

Emmett heard stories from his mother of the letters the widows of Last Chance had sent out after dual blizzards killed most of the town's menfolk. She'd said that it was the machination of Pastor Collins, who insisted the widows remarry or relocate. Emmett had little recollection of Pastor Collins, other than he was an imposing presence and you didn't want to get caught falling asleep during his sermons.

Reminding himself that he was only going to stay here as long as absolutely necessary, Emmett steeled himself and stepped down onto the street. He gritted his teeth as his boot sank ankle deep into a puddle of thick, viscous mud. He pulled his foot loose, careful not to slip with his other one and made his way to the sidewalk. A quick glance down confirmed that his trousers were now splattered with muck too.

He pulled a handkerchief from his pocket, stooped and tried to wipe off some of the offensive mess but only succeeded in smearing it around and making it worse. He rose, sent a quick glare in the stagecoach driver's direction, and shoved the now filthy handkerchief back into his pocket.

Emmett looked across the street and saw that the livery was still where he remembered. A closer look revealed a number of horses inside the structure, and he let out a relieved sigh.

The driver pulled the last of the luggage from the boot, including Emmett's satchel, and tossed the bags in a heap on the sidewalk before Emmett had a chance to take it from him. He grabbed the case from the wet surface, but not before a thin layer of filth lined the bottom of it. The driver gave him a disinterested glance, and walked around to the other side of the stagecoach, out of Emmett's line of vision.

Emmett clenched his jaw and strode down the sidewalk, trying not to notice the squeak his wet boot made with each step. His grip on the handle of his bag tightened until his knuckles were white. The sunless sky was grey and overcast and the earthy scent of wet soil filled the air. Emmett prayed the rain was done as he made his way across the street, mindful of the thick wheel ruts and puddles.

He entered the livery stable and checked to see how much more mud had accumulated on his boots and pants, and hoped they were salvageable. He'd made the mistake of wearing one of his better suits to travel in, hoping to impress his mother when he saw her. Only this was not the kind of impression he'd had in mind.

A tall, dark haired man stepped out from one of the stalls and stared at him through narrowed eyes.

Emmett thought he looked vaguely familiar but couldn't quite place him.

The man's eyebrows lifted. "Emmett Stapleton? Is that you?" He broke into a wide grin and walked toward Emmett, his hand extended in greeting.

Recognition dawned on him as he shook the man's hand. "Dave," he said. Dave McFarland had been one of Wyatt's friends. Dave's family had owned the livery since as far back as Emmett could remember. Dave's father had taken it over for his father, and his father had probably taken it over from Dave's great-grandfather before him.

"I'm sorry about Wyatt," Dave said. "I hear they are doing a memorial service soon. Is that why you're back?"

A strange sensation went through him at the mention of his brother's name. It seemed much easier to not think about Wyatt when he was in Denver, or what had happened between the two of them.

Emmett withdrew his hand and cleared his throat. His mother hadn't mentioned anything in her letters about a memorial service. "I need to rent a horse and buggy," he said, deciding it was best to leave the other man's question unanswered.

Dave hesitated, and for a brief instant Emmett thought he might ask again, but he stepped back and nodded.

"Sure," he said, lifting a harness off a peg on the wall. "I'll get it ready. How long will you need it?"

Emmett thought for a moment. He wasn't sure if his mother still had the old buckboard or not, or how many horses were still on the farm for that matter.

"I'm not sure. Can I have it for the night and let you know tomorrow?"

Dave nodded. "Sure, it rents for one dollar a day." His gaze slid to Emmett's fine suit then back, but he didn't say anything else.

"That will be fine," Emmett said. The rent was less than he'd pay for the same rig in Denver, although he rarely had need to rent one there. Nearly everywhere he went there was within easy walking distance. Mr. Hanna had impressed upon him how important it was not to spend money frivolously. His two legs worked just fine to get him where he needed to go.

Dave hitched a fine looking chestnut mare to the buggy and handed Emmett the reins. Emmett reached for his wallet and Dave held up his hand to stop him.

"Since you don't know how long you'll be needing it," he said. "Just pay when you bring it back."

"Thank you," Emmett replied. He lifted his satchel and settled it on the floor of the buggy, then climbed in.

Dave waved, and Emmett drove out of the livery and down Main Street. The mercantile, Emmett observed with an unexpected touch of nostalgia as he drove past, had not changed at all. He'd spent many hours in the corner of the store, paging through books he only dreamed to one day own.

There was no money for books in the Stapleton home, but Mr. Talley had been sympathetic to the plight of the young boy's yearning for knowledge. He'd agreed to let Emmett read all he wanted out of the books for sale in the store in exchange for weekly cleaning of the stockroom, with the stipulation that the books remained in the store.

That act of kindness opened a door for Emmett that had never closed. His favorite was the Encyclopaedia Britannica. Every time he thought he'd read through everything the store had available, a new volume would show up. When he finished reading those, bound volumes of Chamber's Encyclopaedia appeared on the shelves.

Unfortunately, Emmett's father didn't have the same level of understanding and it created a rift, not only between Emmett and his father, but between his father and Mr. Talley. Emmett shook off the unpleasant thoughts and his attention was drawn to the building adjacent to the mercantile on the other side of the cross street.

The words *Last Chance Savings Bank* were carefully painted on the window facing Main Street. Emmett worked as an assistant cashier at City National Bank back in Denver. He'd worked very hard to get the prestigious job and was proud of it. A banker had connections to all of the important people in the community.

Mr. Hanna was training him for a position as a cashier, but Emmett suspected this leave of absence would prevent any sort of promotion in the near future. Mr. Hanna was not pleased about Emmett's request to return home, even if it was only temporary.

The horse made its way out of town at a brisk pace and in no time, the familiar curve of the barn roof came in to view, creating a hollow sensation in Emmett's chest. He felt his jaw clench tighter and tighter the closer he got. The idea of being back at the place he'd spent nearly a decade to overcome had his stomach churning.

The farm had changed very little since his last visit. A large barn stood across the yard from the house, and provided shelter for the chickens, cows, and horses. A curl of smoke escaped from the chimney of the small log house that, aside from the faded whitewash, appeared to have been well-kept.

A tall, dark-haired young man stepped out of the barn and regarded him with a quizzical expression. Emmett squinted to get a better look. His jaw went slack when he realized the lad was his younger brother, Eli. He was at least a foot taller than the last time Emmett had seen him.

Emmett raised his arm in greeting and watched the boy's eyes grow wide with recognition. He ran toward the house shouting something that Emmett couldn't quite make out. A moment later, as he pulled into the yard and brought the buggy to a stop, his mother stepped out of the house. The trepidation that Emmett felt about coming home left him the moment he saw her.

His mother wore a tan calico print dress with a white apron tied at the waist, and her chestnut brown hair was pulled back into the same, familiar knot she always wore. Emmett noticed it was now shot through with streaks of grey that hadn't been there the last time he'd been home. She was a tall, slender woman with work-worn hands and a warm, gentle smile that lit up her whole face.

"Emmett," she breathed, and rushed toward him.

A lump formed in the back of Emmett's throat as he climbed out of the buggy. She wrapped her arms around him and he pulled her close, inhaling the familiar citrusy scent of her lemon verbena perfume. For a moment, he felt like a child again, safe and snug in her embrace.

She pulled back, placed a hand on either side of his face and stared at him, her blue eyes rimmed with tears.

"Emmett," she cried. "You've come home."

"Mother, it's good to see you," Emmett swallowed down the lump in the back of his throat and reminded himself once again that he was only here temporarily. He took a step back and lifted his satchel out of the buggy. It wouldn't do him any good to let emotions cloud his judgement. Another pearl of wisdom from Mr. Hanna. He had a plan, and it did not involve being in Last Chance any longer than necessary.

Eli walked over and stood next to their mother, folded his arms across his chest, and fixed Emmett with a wary look.

Eli and Wyatt were two people cut out of the same cloth, and Emmett had anticipated a chilly reception from his younger brother. What he hadn't expected was the protective stance the young man had taken over their mother.

"Brother," he said, and offered his hand.

Eli slid a glance at it, but didn't budge.

Emmett raised an eyebrow and let his hand fall to his side.

Their mother gave Eli a disapproving look. "Mind your manners, son."

Eli opened his mouth, but Emmett cut in before he had a chance to speak. "It's fine, Ma," he said, ignoring his brother's glare. He held up his satchel. "Where would you...," he trailed off as a beautiful woman in a soft green gown stepped out of the house.

Her hair was swept into a stylish knot on top of her head. Its deep brown, almost chocolate color, was stunning especially in contrast to her pale skin. She lifted the hem of her skirt and slowly made her way toward them, careful to avoid stepping in one of the many puddles in her path.

Emmett furrowed his brow, unable to recall any mention of a visitor in his mother's letters. When she lifted her gaze and met his, the air went out of his lungs for a moment. He vaguely felt the handle of the satchel slide through his fingers and the dull thud beside him as it hit the ground, but he was unable to pull his attention away from her.

"Oh, Violet, I'm glad you came outside," his mother said from off to his side. "This is my oldest son, Emmett."

Violet? Emmett tried to sort through his muddled thoughts. He couldn't recall ever having met a woman with that name before, and he was relatively certain that he wouldn't have been able to forget her if he had met her.

Violet's arms flailed as she fought to keep her balance. Emmett instinctively stepped forward, but was unable to reach her before she fell face first into the mud.

They stood in shocked silence for a moment as Violet pushed herself up into a sitting position. Out of the corner of his eye, Emmett saw Eli start toward her, but his mother grasped his arm and held him in place.

"Take your brother's satchel into the house," his mother said. "Then come back and get the horse settled into the barn for the night."

"But Ma," Eli grumbled.

A quick look from her quieted any further objection he was about to make. He snatched Emmett's forgotten satchel out of the mud and stomped toward the house.

Emmett glanced down at his fine suit, now splattered with mud, and then at Violet, who sat in a heap in the puddle. He released a slow breath and closed the distance between them.

"Take my hand," he said, and reached toward her. "I'll pull you up."

She looked up at him with wide, deep blue eyes fringed with the longest lashes Emmett had ever seen, and nodded. She placed her small, muddy hand in his and he gave a gentle tug. She rose partway but before she could get her feet under her, Emmett felt her hand slip from his grip and she fell back into the mud.

She made a strange sound and his stomach clenched. *Was she crying?* He hoped not, he had no idea what to do with a crying woman. He reached into his pocket and pulled out his muddy handkerchief.

A giggle rose up from below him. *She was laughing, not crying.* He glanced at his mother, who stood with her hand over her mouth, which Emmett strongly suspected was hiding a snicker.

He shook his head, unable to find any humor in the situation. Right now, the only thing he wanted to do was get out of this dirty, wet suit and see if he could salvage his boots. The muscles in his shoulders and back grew tight.

He looked down at Violet and narrowed his eyes. She pressed her lips together and grew silent. He wasn't sure who this woman was or why she was at his mother's house, but he knew the sooner he got her out of the mud, the sooner he'd be through with her.

He reached down again, this time with both arms. She slid her hands into his without direction and he pulled her to her feet. A soft cry escaped her lips, and she fell against his chest. He wrapped an arm around her waist to keep her from falling.

"What's wrong? Did I hurt you?"

She shook her head. "No, it's my ankle. I must have landed on it wrong when I fell," she looked up at him, her wide eyes full of anguish. Her face was streaked with mud where she'd tried to wipe it, and chunks of mud clung to her hair. "I don't think I can walk on it." Tears filled her eyes, "I'm sorry."

"Bring her into the house," his mother said. "I'll get some ice from the ice house."

Emmett stared at the woman in his arms, unsure where to start. He'd never carried a woman before. It couldn't be much different than picking up a calf, could it?

"I'm going to pick you up," he told Violet, trying to sound confident. "Don't squirm." He bent down and wrapped his arms around her knees and lifted, draping her waist over his shoulder. She pounded on his back.

"This is not how you carry a lady," she cried.

He gripped her legs tighter and strode toward the house. "A lady wouldn't wallow in the mud."

Chapter Three

♥

Emmett pulled the horses to a stop and stared out across the rows of freshly turned soil. He didn't think he would ever finish plowing this section of the field and there was an endless amount of work that awaited him the next day.

The only sounds he heard were birds singing, and the occasional lazy swish of the horses' tails. It was so quiet compared to the cacophony he was used to. There, even at night there was noise. Here, all he heard at night was the rhythmic sound of crickets chirping and the soft sounds of his brother snoring in the bed on the other side of the room. Emmett found the quiet to be somewhat unsettling and much preferred the constant din of the city.

He let out a huff of breath and rolled his stiff shoulders. The homespun fabric of his work clothes was stiff and itchy compared to the fine wool suits he was accustomed to wearing. He looked down at his dirty, blistered hands and shook his head.

It had been a mistake to come here. Mr. Hanna had warned him nothing good would come of going back to one's past. He wished he would have listened.

"Emmett!" a feminine voice called from the far side of the field.

He turned his head to see Violet making her way toward him. She had on a large-brimmed hat that was tied under her chin with a soft pink bow that matched the gown she wore. A dress far more appropriate for a social gathering than for traipsing through the dirt.

After their disastrous meeting, he'd tried his best to avoid her, which was proving to be somewhat difficult given they both stayed in the same house. He could still picture her with muck dripping off her clothes, hair and face, schooling him on the use of mud baths by aristocracy while her aggravating little dog yapped incessantly at his feet.

Her dog was unlike any other Emmett had ever seen. The minuscule creature looked more like a parlor adornment than a living animal. Its silvery-white fur was long and silky, and its tail curled like a plume over its back. It seemed to him that the only thing Violet did during the day was brush the little mongrel, which was why he was so surprised to see her crossing the field.

His chest tightened and his face grew hot as he watched her carefully step over the deep furrows. How one person could exasperate him with a single word was beyond his comprehension, but this woman managed to do just that.

He'd been shocked to discover that she was Wyatt's widow, which then soured into anger and resentment. That his brother had gotten married without his knowledge was bad enough, but the fact that she was still here, months after his death, was preposterous.

His mother insisted she had invited Violet to stay. She explained now that Wyatt was gone, the house was too quiet with just her and Eli, and she enjoyed Violet's company. She said Violet was the daughter she'd never had, but Emmett had his doubts. His mother was firm about the matter, however, and refused to discuss it further.

Eli was completely captivated by her, and continually made a fool of himself trying to impress her. That didn't help the tension growing between the two brothers.

Emmett was determined not to let his relationship with his only remaining brother deteriorate the way his had with Wyatt, but he hadn't figured out how to connect with the boy yet.

As Violet approached, Emmett saw she had a jar of liquid grasped between her hands and his brows lifted. *Was that for him?* He pulled a handkerchief out of his pocket and wiped the sweat from his brow. Though it was only late April, the midday sun was warm and this would be a welcome, though unexpected, break.

She stopped in front of him. Her cheeks flushed a soft pink that matched her dress, and she was slightly out of breath. She was petite with a heart-shaped face, and a dainty nose, and Emmett could see intelligence behind her deep set eyes. He mentally scolded himself for noticing.

"I brought you some switchel," she gave a tentative smile and held out the jar, which contained a clear, amber-colored liquid.

Violet's soft drawl suggested she was from the southern part of the United States. Her mannerisms and dress implied she came from money, or at least had it at one time, as did the large number of trunks he'd found stored in the barn loft.

"Switchel?" Emmett held the jar up to his nose and sniffed. The pungent odor of vinegar was strong, but there was another underlying scent he couldn't identify.

"Yes. Go on, try it," she gestured toward the jar. "It's good."

He cast her a skeptical glance and took a tiny sip, not sure if he should trust her. It was slightly tart, yet sweet and refreshing at the same time. He swallowed more, nearly emptying the jar.

"That is good, thank you. What's in it?" he asked.

"Ginger," she said, and smiled like she had just shared a secret. "It's made with ginger, sugar and vinegar. I learned how to prepare it in Charleston."

He'd been right about where she was from. It made no sense to Emmett that she would travel halfway across the country to marry a simple farmer like Wyatt, and then not return to her people after his death. Especially after such a short time. She was either running away from something or hiding something, he was sure of it.

He studied her for a moment. There was something about her that fascinated him. He scrubbed his hand along his jaw, stubble rough under his fingers. He normally shaved every day, but had gotten out of the habit since he'd been back at the farm.

Emmett could almost hear Mr. Hanna's voice instructing him how a gentleman lets the refinement of his mind and education be seen in his dress. He was suddenly very aware of his soiled, ill-fitted work clothes and unkempt appearance and was glad he at least had a hat to cover his unruly hair.

Why did he care? She blinked and Emmett realized he'd been staring at her too long.

"Charleston," he blurted out, surprising them both. He cleared his throat. "You're from Charleston?" He wasn't sure why he asked except for some reason, he wasn't quite ready for her to leave.

"Yes," she nodded.

"Do you miss it?"

Violet blinked, as if surprised by the question. "I suppose I do." She looked off in the distance for a moment before her gaze returned to him. "Really though, I think it's the familiarities I miss," she said. "The smells and sounds. The things you can't bring with you."

It was Emmett's turn to blink. For someone so young, she was surprisingly insightful.

"It's so quiet here," she continued, and scanned the horizon. "So . . . vast. It's almost primitive."

Emmett followed her gaze. Beyond the field lay miles of what would soon be tall grass and tufts of sage, dotted intermittently with trees and large rocks. He'd never thought of it as primitive, although he could see where someone born and bred in a city might view it that way.

He turned his attention back to her. "What business is your family in?"

Emmett thought he saw a shadow cross her face, but it was gone in an instant, and a wistful smile took its place.

"Trade," she replied. "My father and his business partner had a fleet of clippers they took on trading trips to the Orient and the Mediterranean Sea."

Emmett raised his eyebrows appreciatively. Trade of that nature was a very lucrative profession.

He'd read about the Orient and the countries in the Mediterranean Sea, but the only place besides Last Chance he'd ever been was Denver. He envied Violet of the travel opportunities he'd imagined she had and it made him wonder even more why she would have left that behind.

"It must be difficult to be so far away."

A look of sadness crossed her face and she cast her eyes downward. "Yes," she said in a quiet voice. "I miss him very much."

He pressed his lips together and rubbed his forehead. *It made no sense for her to stay.*

The horses shifted their feet and grunted impatiently, reminding Emmett of the work that needed to be done. He drank the rest of the switchel.

"Thank you," he said and held the jar out toward her.

As she reached for it, her eyes grew wide. She hesitated for a second, then took his hand and turned his palm upward and gasped, running her delicate fingers lightly across the blistered surface.

"Oh my," she exclaimed. "That must be so painful."

He couldn't help but offer a small smile at the concern he heard in her voice, and he met her worried gaze.

"The hands of a banker," he shrugged. Emmett looked at her small, soft hand wrapped around his much larger one and felt a strange warmth spread through him. His head snapped up and he pulled away as if he'd been burned. A smile curved on her lips and her vibrant blue eyes widened as she gazed back at him, causing his breath to catch in his throat.

He took a step back from her and shoved his hands in his pockets. He'd never been affected by a woman in this way.

"I can bandage them when you get back to the house, if you'd like," she offered with a timid smile.

"They'll be fine," he said, his voice sounded gruff to his ears, and he cleared his throat. "Thank you, though."

"I'll prepare a dressing just in case. They really should be wrapped."

Emmett furrowed his brows. No society woman he'd ever met would consider doing such a thing. "Where did you learn about bandaging?"

Indignation flashed in her eyes and her shoulders stiffened. "I *am* educated," she said, her cheeks darkening once again, "and am perfectly capable of making a simple bandage."

Emmett felt heat creep up his neck. "I didn't mean it like that," he said, even though he knew he had. She flustered him, and he wasn't used to that.

She regarded him coolly for a moment, then her expression softened. "I belonged to a club in Charleston called the Young Women's Christian Association. We did a lot of charitable work."

There was a lot more to this woman than he'd expected, and Emmett found himself unsure of how to respond. He wondered again how Wyatt had ended up married to an enigma like her.

Violet rocked on her heels. "I best get back and see if there is anything I can help your mother with," she finally said.

Emmett glanced at the half-plowed field with disdain and nodded. He would never finish the despicable task if he stood here much longer. She gave him a lingering smile, which he hesitantly returned, then she turned and began making her way toward the house with all of his questions still unanswered.

"Violet," Emmett called.

She stopped and turned back to face him, her eyebrows raised.

"Why Wyatt?"

Her eyes widened and her mouth fell open, but no sound came out.

"Why did you marry Wyatt?" Emmett asked again. He had to know.

Violet's face and neck flushed a deep red and her eyes narrowed. "That's really not your concern."

Emmett's shoulders tightened. "He was my brother. That makes it my concern."

She put a hand on her hip. "Your brother didn't even see fit to let you know he was married," she snapped. "If it was truly your concern, you wouldn't need to ask."

He felt his pulse quicken and frowned as the truth behind her words sank in. "Then why did you stay?"

Violet's hand dropped to her side and her flush turned even redder. "I was asked to stay, to make this my home," she stammered.

"What about your own family?"

The jar slipped from her fingers and landed with a dull thud in the dirt, and Violet covered her mouth with her hands. Her eyes filled with tears and Emmett regretted his words. She turned and ran away from him, tripping over the furrowed earth.

The pit in Emmett's stomach grew hard.

"Violet, wait," he called, but she didn't stop. If anything she ran faster. He felt loathsome for making her cry.

Several hours later, with the sun fading in the sky, Emmett led the tired team of horses toward the barn. He was anxious to get himself cleaned up and out of the filthy clothes he wore, and to see if he could make amends with Violet.

The barn door flew open and Eli barreled toward him.

"What did you do to her?" he yelled.

Before Emmett could react, Eli's fist connected with his jaw, snapping his head back. Pain radiated up the side of his face and he took a step back to keep himself from falling.

"What'd you do?"

This time Eli's fist smashed into Emmett's face and he felt the warm trickle of blood running from his nose.

He instinctively lunged toward his younger brother, but Eli dodged to the right. Emmett whirled around and curled his fingers into fists, then froze. *What was he doing? Eli was just a boy.*

He opened his hands and held them up in front of him.

"Eli, stop," he said in as calm and even a tone as he could muster.

Eli opened his mouth and let out a guttural roar as he charged at him. Emmett barely had time to brace himself before the boy crashed into his chest. He seized Eli around the waist, pinning his arms to his sides, and held on tight as the boy kicked and thrashed.

"Let me go!" Eli screamed.

Emmett struggled to keep his grip. "Stop it, Eli. That's enough. I didn't do anything to her."

Eli doubled his efforts to escape and Emmett was amazed at the boy's strength.

"You made her cry," he shouted. "You make everyone cry," he slumped back against Emmett's chest, his breath coming out in ragged sobs. "Why don't you just leave and go back to where you came from," he choked out. "That's what you do best."

Emmett's chest constricted, and his body seemed to crumble under the weight of Eli's words.

"What in heaven's name are you two doing," he heard his mother exclaim, and turned his head to see her running towards them.

He released Eli, who stumbled away from him then ran toward the creek. Emmett watched him disappear into the hollow, then took a deep breath and closed his eyes. *He'd made such a mess of things.*

"Emmett James Stapleton, why are you fighting with your brother?" His mother grasped his arm and turned him so he faced her. He opened his eyes and met her disapproving stare. The anger in her eyes quickly turned into concern as she reached up and tentatively touched his nose.

He flinched, pulled his handkerchief out of his pocket and tried to staunch the blood that still flowed freely down his face. A tight lump formed in the back of his throat as he tried to formulate an explanation. He opened his mouth, but for the second time that day, words failed him.

"Get the horses taken care of and clean yourself up," his mother said. "I'll heat you up some supper, and we'll have us a visit."

Emmett nodded and she patted his arm, then walked back to the house and disappeared inside. He made quick work of unhitching and feeding the horses, who nickered gratefully at the extra bit of hay he gave them.

His nose finally quit bleeding and he stopped at the pump to wash his hands and face. He paused to glance at the tree-lined hollow to see if he could spot any sign of Eli, but there was none. Letting out a long breath, he walked toward the house suddenly feeling like a child that was about to receive his punishment.

Emmett stepped inside and the first thing he noticed was how quiet it was. The second was that neither Violet nor her little dog were anywhere to be seen. *Had she left? What had he done?*

Chapter Four

♥

Violet sat near the fireplace and painstakingly brushed the tangles out of Daisy's fur. The process could sometimes take hours and needed to be done every day. She'd become so used to doing it, she didn't really think much of it anymore.

Stew bubbled on the stove and created an aroma that had Violet's stomach growling in a most unladylike way.

Cora sat across from her in the rocking chair, mending a pair of Eli's trousers. She paused every now and then to stretch out her fingers and Violet noticed for the first time how gnarled and knotty they were.

"If you show me, I can mend those for you," she offered. "I did plenty of embroidery and needlepoint back home." She'd spent hours working on tapestries under the tutelage of her aunt. Violet always considered it a useless skill, but hoped her competence with a needle would be helpful here.

Cora looked up with a smile of thanks. "If you don't mind, that would be wonderful," she cut a glance at the work in her lap. "My fingers don't take to this like they used to, I'm afraid."

Violet grinned, pleased to have found a task she might actually enjoy doing. It wasn't that she was averse to helping, quite the contrary. She just didn't seem to have the aptitude for most of the chores on the farm.

She'd been so grateful when Cora asked her to stay after Wyatt died, but most of the time she felt like a burden because there were so many things she didn't know how to do. Cora had been gracious about it, but Violet was eager to learn more and start earning her keep. Assuming she'd still be able to stay, that is.

She'd spent a restless night locked in her room mulling over her exchange the day before with Emmett. It left her unsettled and fidgety, while doubts about her future took a stronghold.

She worried her bottom lip and held Daisy a little closer. He was going to be trouble for her.

"Are you ready?" Cora asked, pulling Violet out of her reverie. She pulled her chair closer to Cora and watched intently as the older woman demonstrated what to do.

"That looks easy enough," Violet said with an unfamiliar sense of confidence.

"I'll take Daisy for you."

Violet blinked in surprise, placed the dog in Cora's outstretched arms and collected the mending from her lap. Cora had been gracious about allowing Daisy to stay in the house, but she hadn't really paid a lot of attention to the animal up to this point. Violet took it as a good sign.

Daisy, happy with the extra attention, wagged her tail in delight. Cora pulled the animal close to her chest and picked up the small brush.

"Is there any special way to do this?" she asked.

She raised her head and gave Violet a warm smile. "This is quite relaxing," she said. "I can see why you enjoy doing it so often."

Violet returned the smile, and a lightness filled her chest. "It can actually get quite tedious," she admitted, turning her attention to the trousers and pulling the needle in and out like Cora showed her. "But if I don't brush her every day, her fur becomes a snarled mess."

"Oh, I hadn't considered that, but it makes sense," Cora brushed with more confidence now. "You said she was a . . . Maltese?" Cora sounded the word out slowly.

Violet nodded. When she'd first arrived, Cora and Eli had been very curious about what kind of dog Daisy was, having never seen anything like her. Wyatt, on the other hand, barely tolerated her.

"Where did you get her?" Cora asked. "I don't believe you told me."

Violet stopped moving the needle and the back of her throat grew tight. She gazed into Daisy's dark, expressive eyes.

"She was a gift from my father," she said, recalling the joyful expression on his face when he'd handed her the little ball of fur. "He brought her home with him from one of his trips to the Mediterranean."

The brush stilled in Cora's hand. Violet told her that her parents were gone, but had shared little else about her past.

"I understand now why she's so special to you," Cora said softly, and resumed brushing the dog.

The door flew open bringing in a cold gust of air. Violet's stomach tightened as Emmett stepped inside, and she held back a curse as she pierced her own thumb with the needle.

"There's a storm coming," Emmett said, taking off his hat and running his hands through his short, light brown hair. He turned and stopped short as his gaze fixed on the dog nestled on Cora's lap. His brows dipped, but he remained silent and walked to the stove to pour himself a cup of coffee.

Violet's fingers went numb and the needle dropped onto her lap. Her first experience with a storm here in Nebraska had been the horrible blizzards that raged just after she'd arrived. If that's what winter storms were like, she shuddered to think how bad spring storms might be.

"Are the animals all inside?" Cora asked, a note of concern in her voice.

"Yes," he took a sip from the steaming mug. "Eli is checking on the hens, and then he'll be in. Dark clouds are building to the west. I don't like the look of them."

Violet listened intently as Emmett told Cora about the precautions he'd taken. Her heart pounded and she found it difficult to breathe. She pressed a hand to her chest, as though she could slow her racing pulse.

"Is it a c-cyclone?" she sputtered. Just a few years earlier, a tropical cyclone struck Charleston. A cold shiver went through Violet as she recalled the intensity of that storm and the destruction left in its wake, including the flag-stoned walk in High Battery which had been reduced to a pile of rubble.

Cora turned to Violet. "I'm sure it's just a thunderstorm," she said, and leaned forward to give Violet's hand a reassuring squeeze. "Oh my goodness, your hands are freezing cold." She carefully situated Daisy in Violet's arms, and placed the mending back in the basket next to the rocking chair.

"Emmett, bring her some coffee," Cora directed and disappeared into her bedroom. She returned moments later and wrapped a shawl around Violet's shoulders.

Emmett handed her the coffee and Violet wrapped her hands around the warm mug, giving him a grateful smile.

Where Wyatt had been short and rather ordinary, Emmett was tall and despite herself, Violet found him to be incredibly attractive. His eyes were the most unusual mixture of brown and gold, and in them she saw intelligence and curiosity. He had a long, straight nose and square jaw, and kept his face clean shaven.

Violet was torn between wishing he would have stayed in Denver, and being grateful he was here to help the family.

"Are you all right?" he asked. His gaze lingered, and a warmth spread through Violet she was sure didn't have anything to do with the shawl or the coffee.

Unable to find her voice, she nodded and met his intense stare. His behavior confused her. She'd never met anyone who made her feel so vexed, so intrigued and so . . . fluttery. *Stop thinking about him!* She forced herself to look away.

The door opened and Eli burst into the room. He was out of breath and had a wild look in his eyes. Mud caked his trousers and shirt.

"Clarabelle's out," he panted. "I can't find her."

"What do you mean she's out?" Emmett barked. "I locked her up myself."

Eli ran his hands through his wet hair. "I know, I lifted the latch. I - I didn't think...," he cast an anguished glance at Cora. "She ran out-"

Emmett strode to the door, grabbed his hat off the peg and shoved it on his head as he stepped out into the storm.

"I'm sorry, Ma," Eli choked out.

"Go, help your brother," Cora pointed at the open door. "We'll talk about this later."

Eli sniveled and made a gulping noise. "Yes, Ma'am," he said, then turned and ran outside, pulling the door shut behind him.

Violet stared at the door for a moment. She knew Clarabelle was one of the cows, but wasn't sure which one she was. The thought of the poor animal running loose in the storm had tears pooling in her eyes. She turned to Cora.

"Will Clarabelle be safe?" she asked.

"I'm sure she'll be fine," Cora smiled, but Violet could see the worry etched on her face.

Violet glanced down at the forgotten cup of coffee in her hand. She forced herself to take a sip of the nearly tepid liquid, then stood and placed the cup on the table. She didn't want to seem ungrateful, but no matter how hard she tried to like it, she just didn't have a taste for it.

Violet much preferred tea, and had been pleasantly surprised at the variety of flavors the mercantile carried. Cora, however, preferred coffee, and out of respect for the lady of the house, Violet deferred to her preference.

Thunder crashed overhead and Daisy trembled in her arms. Violet pulled her inside the shawl, not caring what kind of mess it would make of her long coat, and returned to her chair. She whispered words of reassurance in the dog's tiny ear, hoping they might calm her own nerves as well.

"You really love Daisy, don't you?"

Violet stiffened and felt her cheeks grow hot. Her Aunt Dorcas ridiculed her daily for the amount of attention lavished on the dog. She studied Cora's eyes, but detected no malice in them, and her shoulders relaxed a bit.

"I do," she said. "She's really all I have."

"Well now you have us, too," Cora smiled gently.

A lump formed in the back of Violet's throat and her vision blurred. She lowered her head and buried her face in Daisy's soft fur and prayed with all her might that Cora spoke the truth.

Another clap of thunder shook the house. Violet jumped, and Cora rose and hurried to the windows to fasten the shutters. The wind picked up and it made an eerie howling sound, and the pit-a-pat of rain hitting the roof turned into sharp, staccato drumming that grew so loud Daisy began to howl.

Violet's heart hammered in her chest and her breath caught in her throat. She turned to Cora with a questioning look.

"Hail," Cora said, and rubbed her hands up and down her arms as she paced in front of the fireplace. "It's hailing."

Violet closed her eyes and tried to slow her breathing. If they needed to take shelter, Cora would tell her, she reasoned. But where would they go? Violet mentally scanned the farm. She didn't think the barn would be any safer than the house, but perhaps the root cellar. The barn . . . Clarabelle . . .

Her eyes snapped open. "Emmett," she gasped, covering her mouth with her hand.

"They'll be fine," Cora said, but Violet could hear a catch in her voice.

Violet closed her eyes again, her fingers methodically stroking Daisy's fur.

Heavenly Father, protect Emmett and Eli from the storm. Please keep them safe. She repeated the prayer over and over in her mind.

The minutes ticked by as the storm raged outside. The hammering of the hail on the roof subsided, and once again became the soft patter of rain. The wind died down and ceased its howling.

Cora returned to the window and peered through it, rubbing her hands up and down her arms. A knot formed in Violet's stomach. Why weren't they back yet?

"Oh goodness!" Cora ran to the door and pulled it open. Violet sat forward on her chair, her eyes wide. It looked like it had snowed. The ground was covered in a blanket of hail, some of which were nearly the size of her fist.

Emmett and Eli stumbled into the house. Eli's arm was around Emmett's waist and Emmett held a hand to his head. Violet could see blood streaming through his fingers and down the side of his face. They were both soaked through, and water pooled on the floor where they stood.

"Violet, get some towels," Cora said, and led Emmett to one of the chairs. Violet stared at them, unable to move, or think.

Cora turned to her. "Violet," she repeated. "Towels, please."

Violet looked at her for a moment as the words tumbled through her head. Towels, of course! She placed Daisy on her cushion and ran into the other room. She returned a moment later and handed a clean towel to Cora, who was examining the wound on Emmett's head.

Violet handed the other towel to Eli, who stood shivering by the door, looking as though he were about to burst into tears.

Cora dabbed at the gash on Emmett's forehead and he winced. Violet pressed a hand across her chest. It looked so deep.

"Shall I run and get the doctor?" she offered, and heard a strangled sob come from behind her where Eli stood.

"No," Cora and Emmett said at the same time.

"I'll be able to bandage it, I think," Cora said. "What happened?"

"We found Clarabelle down in the hollow," Emmett said. "We were just about back when the wind picked up."

Violet gasped. "Did you get struck by hail?"

"No, I think it was a shingle from the barn roof," he said with a note of disgust. "Several shingles flew off. The roof is going to need to be repaired."

"I'll do it," Eli chimed in.

Cora looked over her shoulder at her youngest son. "You will do no such thing," she said. "Now go and change into some dry clothes before you catch a cold."

"But, Ma," Eli pleaded.

"Go," Cora waved toward the ladder that led to the large loft room that Eli and Emmett shared. Eli furrowed his brow and opened his mouth as though he was going to say something, but Cora narrowed her eyes at him, and he snapped his mouth shut and climbed into the loft without a word.

Violet watched the interplay between mother and sons with great interest. She'd been just a few years younger than Eli when her own mother died, and she had no siblings. After that, it had just been her and her Aunt Dorcas. Aunt Dorcas was a spinster who had no motherly qualities whatsoever.

An image of her mother focused in Violet's memory. As a child, Violet thought her mother to be the most beautiful woman in the world. She would pretend her mother was a queen and that her father was off on adventures to slay dragons to protect them, instead of merchant trips. Because her father was gone for long periods of time, Violet and her mother were very close.

Her mother had wanted a whole house full of children, but when only Violet came, she doted on her. If Violet closed her eyes, she could still hear her mother's soft voice. *How's my little flower petal?* The back of her throat tightened and Violet pushed the memories out of her head. Maybe if she kept herself busy, her mind wouldn't wander.

She retrieved a piece of muslin from Cora's scrap box, tore it into strips to be used as a bandage, and then brought Cora a basin of water. Cora gave her a grateful smile, and Violet stood a bit straighter.

"Was Clarabelle the only one that got out?" Cora asked, pressing the towel against the wound on Emmett's head to staunch the bleeding.

"Yes," Emmett said. "Eli's lucky the Herefords' didn't get loose. There's one due to calve any day."

"Calve?" Violet frowned. "Does that mean it's going to have a baby?"

Emmett and Cora both looked at her and blinked. Violet felt a rush of heat go up her neck and across her cheeks. She wished she had kept her question to herself. Dorcas always told her she was too inquisitive.

"Yes," Emmett finally said. "There are two bred heifers in the lot," he explained. "One is due to have her calf any day, and the other later this month." His tone was pleasant, not condescending or mocking, and Violet offered him a grateful smile.

"Did he say why he opened the gate latch?" Cora asked.

Emmett's lips pressed tightly together as Cora dabbed at the wound on his head again. "He knew I locked them up and wanted to make it look like I was the one that left it open. When Clarabelle got loose, he panicked."

Cora shook her head. "You boys need to mend your fence."

Violet's brow lifted. She'd never heard that expression before.

"He's the one with the attitude," Emmett said. "You've spoiled him." He tried to stand. Cora placed a hand on his shoulder and pushed him back on to the chair.

"Let me finish," she chided. "He may have more liberties than you did, but he also works much harder than most boys, including you when you were that age." She gave Emmett a pointed look.

He glanced at Violet and she was sure she saw a bit of pink color his face.

"It was hard for him when you left," Cora continued. "He adored you."

"He was five," Emmett countered.

"And you were his big brother."

Violet chewed her bottom lip. She felt as though she was eavesdropping on a conversation that ought to be private. She looked around the room and her gaze settled on the steaming pot of stew. Perfect!

"Cora," she said, and clasped her hands in front of her. "Would you like me to make biscuits for the stew?"

"That would be wonderful, Violet. Thank you."

Violet practically skipped to the kitchen, eager to try her hand at baking. She pulled Cora's mixing bowl down and assembled the ingredients. She'd watched Cora prepare them a number of times, and was confident she'd be able to replicate them.

The dough came together with ease, and Violet grinned as she dropped it onto the floured counter. She dusted her hands with flour and kneaded the dough until it was smooth. Then she rolled it out and cut it into circles with a glass dipped into flour, just like Cora did. She placed them in the cast iron pan and admired them for a moment before sticking the pan in the oven.

By the time the biscuits were ready, Cora had finished bandaging Emmett's head and Eli had come down from the loft. Violet set the table and felt her chest swell a bit as she looked at the golden brown biscuits piled high on a plate in the center.

They said grace and as Violet watched Cora fill their bowls with rich, brown stew, an unexpected ache filled her heart.

"Oh, Emmett," Cora said as she handed the last bowl to Eli and settled in her chair. "I meant to thank you for the extra help since . . . ," she paused and a flicker of sadness crossed her face.

Violet's breath caught in her throat and the spoon fell from her hand onto the table with a clatter. Her heart raced and she was sure at any moment it would leap straight out of her chest.

Emmett frowned. "What -" Emmett began, but Violet cut him off.

"Yes, Emmett. Thank you." She needed a diversion, fast. She searched the table for something. Anything. Her gaze settled on the water pitcher and she sprang to her feet. "Let me get you some water," she said, trying to keep her voice steady.

She grabbed the cup in front of Emmett and hastily filled it. He nodded his thanks and turned back to his mother with a look of confusion on his face. Violet's chest grew tight and her throat constricted as Emmett opened his mouth to speak.

"Here you go." Her voice sounded shrill to her own ears. Emmett pressed his lips together and reached out his hand. Violet thrust the full cup toward him. It ricocheted off his fingers and she let it slip from her hand, grimacing as it landed on the table with a clatter, spilling its contents directly onto Emmett's lap.

Letting out a yelp of surprise, Emmett shoved his chair back and stood. Water ran in rivulets down the front of his trousers.

"Oh goodness," Violet cried. "Let me get a towel." She ran into the kitchen and grabbed a couple of towels. Waves of guilt washed over her as she handed it to Emmett and watched him dab at the soaked fabric. She glanced at the table and let out a quick sigh of relief when she saw that no water had spilled on the biscuits.

"I'm so sorry," she said, sopping up the water on the floor with the extra towel.

"No harm done," Cora said. "It's just water."

By the time Emmett dried his pants enough to return to his chair, the conversation about the extra money appeared to have been forgotten, at least temporarily. Just to be sure, Violet turned to Emmett.

"Emmett, would you please tell me what Denver is like? I read about the mountains in Colorado. Have you seen them?"

Eli reached for a biscuit and shoved it into his mouth. He winced in pain and spit it onto his plate.

Violet frowned. Perhaps it's just too hot, she reasoned.

"What did you do to the biscuits?" Eli rubbed his jaw dramatically. "They're hard as a rock!"

Chapter Five

♥

Emmett hit the nail with the hammer one last time, driving it the rest of the way into the board. He took a few steps back and surveyed his work. He'd spent the better part of the last week repairing damage to the house and barn and cleaning up debris after the storm.

At the end of each day, his muscles were sore and he was so tired he sometimes felt as though he didn't have the strength to climb the ladder into the loft. But as he looked at the newly repaired barn wall, his chest swelled with a sense of accomplishment.

Emmett loved working at the bank, but, as much as he hated to admit it, there was a difference in being able to see the results of your hard work with your own eyes rather than as a total at the bottom of a column of numbers.

A movement near the house caught his attention and he turned to look. Violet. She crossed the yard toward the barn with a pensive expression on her face. She was so focused on where she was going that she didn't appear to notice he was standing there. What was she up to?

Emmett rubbed his jaw, recalling the conversation he'd had with his mother the night before the storm. He felt awful about hurting Violet's feelings that day by asking her why she hadn't returned to her family after Wyatt's death. He felt even worse when his mother told him that her parents were both gone.

Since then, he'd observed how hard Violet tried to help his mother with chores in the house. She struggled with what he considered simple tasks, and she was an awful cook, but he could see she was making a genuine effort to help.

He wondered again why Wyatt would have chosen someone so unlike him to marry. He was an impatient man on the best of days, one of the many reasons they didn't get along. Emmett couldn't imagine him being patient with Violet while she tried to learn.

Wyatt wasn't one for show, either. He couldn't have liked Violet's fancy city clothes, or her charm and refinement. She was a peacock and, in Emmett's opinion, Wyatt would have been much better suited to a pigeon.

His mother really seemed to enjoy her presence though. He noticed his mother didn't stand quite as straight as she used to. Her hair, once a rich caramel brown, was now streaked with grey, and more than once he'd seen her massaging knots out of her hands, although she never complained about them.

Having Violet there allowed her to rest a bit more, and Emmett was grateful for that. It would make going back to Denver easier. He'd received a telegram from Mr. Hanna, who was getting impatient for his return, and Emmett had replied, asking for more time.

Thankfully, the hail storm came through before any of the crops emerged. That saved Emmett from having to replant, but there was still a lot of work to be done before he could leave.

Violet stopped by the corral and stared at the cattle for a moment before stepping into the barn. She emerged a minute later with the milk bucket draped over one arm. Emmett watched with great interest as she started toward the pen at the far end of the corral.

Emmett walked up to the corral fence and leaned across it with both arms and watched her. She was wearing a light purple gown today with a dark purple sash tied at the waist, and she had one of his mother's bonnets on her head. The combination, which should have been hideous, somehow seemed to look quite normal on her.

He waited until she reached the gate before he spoke. "What are you doing?"

Violet gasped and spun around to face him. She splayed a hand across her chest and frowned at him.

"Emmett! You scared me half to death. Don't you know it's not polite to sneak up on a lady?"

"The lady in question walked right past me," he said, and a smile tugged at the corner of his mouth. "I would hardly consider that to be sneaking."

Violet tilted her head to one side and lifted a brow. "You should still have made your presence known," she admonished him, but Emmett could see a twinkle of mischief in her eyes.

He straightened, then placed an arm across his waist and bowed low. "Please accept my sincerest apologies."

She laughed. Her laugh was just like the rest of her, Emmett noted. Sweet and genuine. He blinked. Where did that come from? He gave himself a mental shake.

"Where are you going with that?" he gave a nod toward the pail she still carried on her arm.

She slid a quick glance down and then back to him. "Why, to milk Clarabelle, of course," she said, waving her free hand at the animal in the pen. "Your mother asked me if I might help," she said with a proud smile.

Emmett's mouth twitched as he tried to hold back the laughter that bubbled inside his chest. Violet's brows knit together as she frowned.

"I fail to see what you find so amusing about the simple task of milking a cow." She lifted her chin and narrowed her eyes at him.

"I don't find milking a cow to be amusing in the least."

She smoothed the front of her skirt with a sharp motion of her hand, and tossed her head. "Well then, if you'll excuse me," she said, and reached for the latch on the gate.

"What I find amusing," Emmett called after her, trying desperately to keep a straight face. "What exactly is it you plan to do with that bull?"

Violet's hand froze. Her eyes widened, and her mouth opened forming a small "O". Her gaze flitted between him and the bull, and she took a quick step back from the gate.

"B-bull? But Cora said it was the cow all by itself," she shot a quick glance at the bull. "It's by itself," she said, and took another step back as the large animal turned and pressed its nose against the gate.

"Clarabelle is by herself," Emmett smirked. "Inside the barn."

A flush began in her cheeks, and spread across her nose into her ears, and finally down her neck until her whole face was bright red. Her bottom lip trembled, and Emmett's chest grew tight as tears welled in her eyes. Then something in her expression changed. Her jaw tightened and she balled her hands into fists.

She stomped her foot. "Emmett Stapleton, you are an incorrigible rogue!" She brushed past him and marched toward the barn. He stood in stunned silence as he watched Violet move away from him, her back rigid and her arms swinging by her side, the pail clenched tightly in one hand.

A slow smile spread across Emmett's face as he trailed after her. He'd never met a woman that spoke as freely as Violet. She was spunky, and sassy, and . . . beautiful.

He followed her into the barn, although he couldn't say why exactly. He had plenty of work to keep him busy outside. He reminded himself that he was going back to Denver soon and didn't need to waste his time with this kind of distraction. But, nevertheless he found himself inexplicably drawn to her.

Emmett found her standing outside of Clarabelle's stall, staring at the cow as though she'd never seen one before. Maybe she hadn't before coming to Nebraska. He couldn't imagine there were cows wandering through the streets of Charleston.

"What are you doing here?" Violet asked, glaring at him. He was still trying to figure that out himself. When he didn't immediately respond, she continued. "Are you here to further amuse yourself with my ineptitude?"

Emmett's jaw dropped and a small chuckle escaped his lips. He'd never met a woman that could render him speechless, yet Violet somehow had a knack for it.

Violet let out a huff of irritation. "Contrary to what you may think, I am perfectly capable of handling this without your help, or your commentary," she said, and turned her back on him. She undid the latch and pulled open the door of the stall, then hesitated.

Emmett crossed his arms over his chest and leaned back against the wall of the adjacent stall.

He wasn't ready to leave quite yet. Part of him felt like he owed her an apology for not stopping her as soon as he realized her mistake with the bull. The other part of him was curious to see if she actually could milk a cow.

Clarabelle uttered a soft moo and took a step toward the open stall door. Violet gasped and leaped back, covering her mouth with her free hand.

"Will she bite?" she asked through her fingers, not taking her eyes off the cow. Clarabelle stared back at her, calmly chewing her cud and occasionally swishing her tail.

Emmett bit back a smile. "No. That feather duster of yours would bite you before that cow would."

Violet shot an icy glare over her shoulder at him. "Feather duster?!" She stomped her foot on the ground. "Daisy is a sweet, well-tempered little dog that wouldn't harm a fly. I'm not sure I could say the same about you, however." She took a step closer to Clarabelle, and tentatively held her hand just a few inches from the cow's nose.

The black and white cow lifted her head and nudged Violet's hand. Violet ran her hand up her nose, between her eyes, and gave her a scratch on the forehead. Clarabelle closed her eyes and gave a contented moo. Violet flashed Emmett a triumphant grin and stepped into the stall.

From his vantage point by the stall's door, Emmett watched the twist of Violet's lips and determined furrow of concentration on her forehead as she studied the cow. She gingerly placed the pail beneath the animal and stepped back.

Violet stared at the pail for a long moment, then brought her hand up and rubbed her lips with her fingers while she thought. She adjusted the pail a few inches and stepped back again, resting her hands on her hips. After a minute, she let out an exasperated sigh and turned to Emmett.

"Why won't the milk come out?"

Emmett regarded Violet with amusement for a split second until he realized she was serious. He suppressed the urge to chuckle and stepped into the stall. He pulled the milk stool from the corner and placed it next to Clarabelle.

"Let me show you," he said, and indicated she should sit. She gave him a bemused stare, but settled herself on the stool.

He crouched next to her, and detected the soft floral scent of the cologne she wore. Or maybe it was her hair. The temperature in the barn seemed to raise several degrees and he wiped his clammy hands on the front of his trousers.

Clarabelle swished her tail impatiently, forcing Emmett's attention back to the task in front of him. He placed the pail directly under her udder.

"Watch how I do it," he said. A moment later, fresh milk streamed into the pail. He turned to Violet. Her deep blue eyes were wide and unblinking, her mouth slightly open. She slid him a guarded look.

"Doesn't that hurt her?"

"No," he said, and a smile tugged at the edge of his mouth. "It actually makes her feel good. If she goes too long between milkings, she gets sore."

She stared back at him as though she wasn't sure if she should believe him, but then nodded.

"You try," he sat back a bit to give her more room.

"Oh, I couldn't." She frowned and put her hands together under her neck.

"Sure you can," he encouraged her.

Violet gave him a wary glance, cautiously lowered her hand, and tentatively reached under the cow. She gave a timid squeeze and when no milk swished into the pail, she looked up at Emmett.

"I can't do it," she said, and her eyes filled with tears. Emmett could hear the defeat in her voice. She lowered her head and her shoulders sagged.

He frowned. This was so unlike the woman who very handily put him in his place just a few minutes earlier. Then he remembered the night of the storm. She'd reacted the same way over the failed biscuits.

Emmett didn't know much about her past, other than that her parents were both deceased. He was beginning to wonder what happened that made her so insecure about her abilities, and decided to make sure this experience was a success for her.

"I didn't get milk to come out my first time either," he admitted. Her head snapped up and she gazed at him from under the brim of the bonnet, her eyes damp with tears.

"Really?" She sniffed.

"Really," he said. "Try again, I'll show you."

She reached back under the cow and Emmett placed his hand over hers. He felt a flutter in his stomach and drew in a long, slow breath. Focus! He turned his attention back to the cow, and demonstrated how to squeeze and pull at the same time. A swish of milk streamed into the pail.

"Now you try," he reluctantly removed his hand and sat back on his heels. Violet took a deep breath and repeated the technique he'd shown her, and another stream of milk landed in the pail.

"I did it!" She looked up at him and her whole face lit up. Then she laughed, a wonderful, joyous sound, and in that moment, Emmett knew he was lost.

Several hours later, Emmett held a cup of coffee in his hands and stared into the dying embers of the fire. His mother had brought home another telegram from Mr. Hanna. His patience was wearing thin and he demanded Emmett return to Denver the following week, or risk losing the job he'd worked so hard to get.

Emmett sighed. There was much work that still needed to be done on the farm. He glanced across the room where his mother and Violet sat across from each other at the table. They both worked on sewing projects, and Emmett couldn't help but smile as he heard his mother laugh at something Violet had said.

Daisy perched herself at the foot of Emmett's chair, and stared up at him. Her dark eyes blinked at him like two black buttons on a pile of snow. Her long white fur flowed down her back and lay in wisps alongside her on the floor.

Despite the fact that he'd paid no attention to the animal, she seemed to be enamored with him and was constantly underfoot when he was in the house. He slid a quick glance at the table, and once he was sure neither of the women were looking, he reached down and gave the dog a quick pat on her head.

Emmett placed his coffee on the table beside him and leaned forward, resting his elbows on his knees. He looked down at the callouses that had replaced the blisters on his hands and thought again about Mr. Hanna's message. Deep down, he knew farming wasn't the kind of life he wanted, but as he listened to the laughter coming from the women at the table, he wasn't so sure he was ready to leave it behind either.

Chapter Six

♥

Violet tried not to focus on the way the light pressure of Emmett's hand on the small of her back made her stomach flutter as he gently guided her through Dawson's Diner to a table in the corner.

She was used to the curious stares from people in town, but it seemed that the two of them together were drawing more interest than usual.

Emmett must have sensed her discomfort. "It's perfectly acceptable for me to dine with my brother's wife," he assured her, a little louder than necessary. Violet couldn't help glancing around the room, but when no other eyes met hers, she relaxed a bit.

He held up the menu. "Have you eaten here before?"

Violet shook her head and studied the menu in front of her. The menu contained many of the same dishes that Cora cooked, as well as several items she wasn't familiar with. The aromas wafting out from the kitchen were tantalizing, and she was confident that everything listed would be delicious.

When she lived in Charleston, dining out was a regular occurrence. There it was more about who you were with and who might see you than actually dining. In fact, many times after such a meal, she'd wait until her aunt retired for the night, then sneak into the kitchen for a little snack.

The waitress came and took their orders and after she left, Emmett's words played through Violet's mind. *My brother's wife.* The words formed a lump in the back of her throat and she took a sip of cool water from the glass in front of her to wash them back down.

Earlier in the day, when Emmett asked her if she would accompany him to town, Violet had readily agreed. She'd taken extra care with her hair and had selected a dove grey gown she knew brought out the blue in her eyes. She'd even pinched a bit of color into her cheeks. Now she felt rather foolish for even thinking that he'd been paying her special attention. He was so different from Wyatt.

Violet had barely known Wyatt before he'd been killed. Certainly not long enough to have fallen in love with him. Their union had been little more than a marriage of convenience. He needed a wife to help his mother on the farm, and she needed safety. What could be safer than a farm in an obscure little town in the middle of Nebraska?

Would she have grown to love him? She would never know, but the more she learned about

Wyatt, the more incompatible she thought they would have been. Reminding herself it was gauche to think ill of the dead, Violet took another quick glance around the diner.

She recognized several people, but many she'd never seen before. A movement by the door drew her attention. A short, thin man wearing a dark suit and stovepipe hat entered the dining room. He made his way to a table by the window, adjacent to the one she shared with Emmett.

There was a certain air of authority about him. A knot started to form in the pit of Violet's stomach. The man placed his hat on the table and removed his frock, and that's when she saw the badge pinned to his waistcoat. A Pinkerton badge. Why was a Pinkerton detective in Last Chance? Violet's mind raced as she tried to come up with a reason that didn't involve her.

She'd been careful since her arrival to spend as little time in town as necessary, making only occasional trips to the Mercantile and the bank.

The bank. Of course. She let out a frustrated sigh. *How could she be so naive?* Surely, her Aunt Dorcas wouldn't go to such lengths to find her, would she? *No.* Violet tried to calm herself. *She was just being overly suspicious.*

"A penny for your thoughts," Emmett's voice drew Violet out of her musings. He stared at her from across the table with a grin of amusement.

Heat crept up her neck and across her cheeks. "You must forgive my rudeness," she said, and offered him a smile, and forced her attention from the agent. "It's been some time since I've been in a restaurant."

"I wish I could say the same," Emmett said, then shook his head. "I didn't mean it like that. If the food here is as good as it smells, I'm sure we are in for a treat. But after eating nearly every meal for the last decade in a restaurant, it's been nice to have home-cooked food too."

"We had a cook back in Charleston," Violet said, then let out a little laugh. "Now you know the reason for my culinary incompetence."

"I'd argue that point, but I did eat one of your biscuits," he said with a chuckle. "Or at least I tried to."

The waitress appeared with their food and Emmett asked her to bring them each a tall glass of lemonade. Violet perked up, she loved lemonade and it had been a long while since she'd had any. Her Aunt Dorcas didn't care for it and therefore, wouldn't allow it in the house. But her father had loved it. Violet's vision clouded for a moment and she blinked the memory away.

They spent the remainder of the meal chatting about the many differences between living on the farm and living in the city, and Emmett had many questions about the ocean. The food was delightful, and when they finished their meal and got up to leave, Violet was relieved to see the Pinkerton agent was gone.

They stepped out into the street. The midday sun was warm for early May, and Emmett suggested a walk might be nice. Violet agreed, and when he offered his arm, she gave a smile and threaded her gloved hand through the crook of his elbow.

Emmett was considerably taller than Violet, but it was even more apparent to her as she walked by his side. Even with her heeled boots, there was still nearly a foot difference in their height. They strolled up Stagecoach Road and Emmett made several comments about the changes that had taken place since he'd last been home.

As they neared the intersection at Main Street, Violet noticed a man lurching toward them. She squinted to get a better look and stiffened when she recognized him. *Otis Ignatius Graham.*

Emmett must have felt her reaction, because he followed her gaze. "Well, I'll be," he muttered. "Old Otis is still around."

Violet sniffed and tightened her grip on Emmett's elbow, the memory of her last encounter with the old man still clear in her mind. He stumbled closer and Emmett stopped. He pulled a bill out of his pocket and handed it to Otis as he passed by.

"Here you go, Otis. Get yourself something to eat."

"My name is *Otis Ignatius Graham*," Otis slurred, and held the bill up close to his face. He squinted up his eyes, then held it at arm's length and studied it. Violet half expected him to stick it in his mouth next, but he shoved it in his pocket instead and continued down the street without another word.

"You know him?" she asked Emmett once she was certain Otis was out of earshot.

"Everyone knows Otis," he said. "He's been that way as long as I can remember. I take it you've met him?"

"In a manner of speaking," she said, unable to hide the scorn in her voice. She explained to him what happened the last time she'd encountered

Otis. When Emmett burst out laughing, Violet joined him. It did seem rather humorous now.

"I'm sure he didn't mean to offend you. He had probably never seen a calling card before and had no idea what it was. He's a harmless half-wit."

Violet looked up at him and quirked her brow. "Would that be more or less harmless than a whole-wit?"

Emmett's eyes widened in surprised amusement at her quip, and he laughed again.

"Violet, you are a breath of fresh air," he covered her hand resting in the crook of his elbow with his and gave her fingers a light squeeze. "It's becoming very apparent to me why my mother enjoys your presence so much."

She did? Violet turned her head so he wouldn't see the tears that were gathering in her eyes. Her aunt made no secret of the fact that she considered Violet a nuisance. A burden she bore out of obligation to her brother, nothing more. It had been a very long time since Violet felt like she belonged somewhere. Dare she believe him?

"Would you like a Sarsaparilla?" Emmett gestured toward the Mercantile. "When I was here last week, I noticed Mr. Talley unpacking a box of bottles."

Violet quickly dabbed her eyes with her gloved fingers.

"Oh yes," she exclaimed, turning her head back toward him. "I would love that. I haven't had a Sarsaparilla since," she scrunched her nose while she thought. "Well, I can't even remember the last time. Thank you, Emmett."

He smiled down at her and his gaze lingered, causing a flutter of butterflies to take flight in her stomach. Looking up at him, Violet didn't think she'd ever seen a more handsome man. She suddenly found herself wondering what it would be like to kiss him.

Heat flooded her neck and face and she abruptly turned away. *Where did that come from?*

She had never even kissed a man before, not even Wyatt. He'd given her a perfunctory peck on the cheek at their nuptial ceremony, of course, but she didn't think that counted as a real kiss. He'd told her he was in no hurry to rush into their marriage bed, and they would discuss such issues upon his return from the ill-fated hunting trip.

But there was something different about Emmett, or maybe it was the way he looked at her that was different. She saw something in his eyes that made her wonder if maybe, just maybe he did think she was special.

She allowed him to guide her into the Mercantile, enjoying the possessive feel of his hand on her back.

Phyllis Talley was engaged in a lively conversation with Penelope Purcell at the end of the counter when they walked into the store. Penelope glanced in their direction and stopped talking mid-sentence, but her mouth still hung open. Her gaze flitted to Emmett's hand, which remained on Violet's back, and her eyebrows lifted.

Phyllis nudged Penelope with her elbow and Penelope's mouth snapped shut with an audible click. Violet suppressed a shudder. Penelope reminded her of her Aunt Dorcas's friend, Lucinda. Dorcas and Lucinda had tea together nearly every afternoon and would blather on about nearly everyone in Charleston.

The last thing Violet wanted was to be fodder for gossip. *But you haven't done anything wrong.* The words Emmett spoke at the diner echoed through her mind again, and she lifted her chin. She looked Penelope right in the eyes and gave her a polite nod.

Phyllis gave Violet a warm smile as she and Emmett stepped up to the counter. "Violet, how wonderful to see you again. I'm sorry I missed you the last time you were in. You look positively radiant. That gown is stunning" she said, and turned to Emmett. "Don't you agree, Emmett?"

Emmett tilted his head as he looked at Violet, and the corner of his mouth lifted into a gentle smile.

"The beauty of the gown is merely enhanced by the woman wearing it."

Violet stared back at Emmett in stunned silence. She'd never had a man speak that way about her. Her fingers creased the front of her gown as a shy smile crossed her lips. She repeated his words in her mind so she would always remember them, remember this day.

The bell over the door chimed and reminded Violet where she was. She turned to Phyllis who stared back at her, amusement clear on her face, and felt heat flush her cheeks.

"I'd like two bottles of Sarsaparilla, please." Emmett's deep voice broke the silence, and Violet was grateful for the diversion.

Struck with a sudden idea, she looked at Emmett. "Can we get a bottle for Eli, too?"

Emmett's brow raised. "That's a fine idea," he swung his gaze back to Phyllis. "Make that three."

Phyllis opened two of the bottles and handed one to each of them, and placed the unopened one in front of Emmett, who promptly placed it in the inner pocket of his frock coat. He placed a coin on a counter and after bidding the women a good day, they left the store.

"Thank you for the treat," she said as Emmett guided her down the stairs and onto the sidewalk, then added, "and for getting a bottle for Eli." She threaded her hand back through the crook of his elbow and they began to walk back toward Stagecoach Road.

Emmett shrugged and took a sip from his bottle. Violet studied him for a moment. He was a proud man who stood behind his beliefs. Eli was the same way. She knew the discord between the two of them troubled Cora, but didn't know if it was her place to get involved.

"What?" Emmett asked, raising a brow.

Violet frowned, but before she could ask him what he meant, he continued. "I can see you want to say something," he said, the corners of his mouth lifting in an amused smirk. "You may as well just come out with it."

Heat crept into her cheeks and Violet took a sip from her bottle, letting the sweet, cool liquid slide down her throat.

"I thought it might be a good way for you to engage Eli in conversation," she finally said, lifting one shoulder and giving him a hopeful smile.

He snorted. "It's unlikely a Sarsaparilla is going to mend that fence," he replied, using his mother's words.

Violet pressed her lips together, gave him a sidelong stare and let out an indignant sigh. "Well, you have to start somewhere," she said. "It won't mend itself."

Emmett regarded her with a look of blithesome curiosity. "You may have a small point," he conceded.

Violet was about to respond when out of the corner of her eye she recognized Pastor Collins as he hurried across the street towards them. *Maybe he's going to the Mercantile*, she tried to tell herself, but the hairs on the back of her neck stood on end when he stopped in front of them.

"Ahh, Mr. Stapleton and Mrs. Stapleton," he greeted, as a polite smile curved his thin lips.

A shiver ran down Violet's spine, despite the warm breeze. There was something about the pastor that gave her the creeps, something she couldn't quite put into words. His black, flat brim hat was pulled down low on his forehead and he wore his usual black frock.

Barnaby Collins's moralizing about God being angry and punishing the town by sending the blizzards didn't align with the lessons Violet had been taught about God as a child. Nor did she agree with his insistence that all the widows in town remarry or relocate.

Times were changing. Her mother, who was a member of the South Carolina Woman Suffrage Association, had believed that women were equal to men and thus, should have the same rights. Her mother had even met Susan B. Anthony and Elizabeth Cady Stanton at a women's rights convention, and she'd strived to instill those beliefs in her daughter.

Her Aunt Dorcas, however, was a staunch opponent of the suffrage movement. She believed a woman's place in society was running the household and being involved in charitable, philanthropic and educational activities, but not in politics.

On one hand, Violet could appreciate that the preacher thought he was doing the right thing, but on the other, Violet thought it was unfair for Pastor Collins to demand such drastic measures. Most of the women in Last Chance hadn't even been allowed time to properly mourn. She'd managed to successfully avoid a direct conversation with him up until now, but she didn't think she'd get out of it this time.

His small eyes focused on her and she let out a pent up breath as he turned to Emmett and touched the brim of his hat with his long fingers.

"Pastor Collins," Emmett nodded a return greeting and attempted to step around him, but he made a quick sidestep and blocked his path.

"Mr. Stapleton, how good to see you've finally come home to look after your family," Pastor Collins said. "I'd begun to wonder if you were ever going to return."

Violet felt the muscles in Emmett's arm tighten under her hand.

"And Mrs. Stapleton," Pastor Collins directed his attention to her. He cast a disapproving glance at her gown, and his upper lip curled in a sneer. *What was wrong with her dress?* Granted, it wasn't the same, simple calico that most of the women in Last Chance wore, but it was far from risqué. The Sarsaparilla Violet drank just a few minutes earlier now burbled in her stomach.

"When can I expect you at the church to exchange holy vows?" His eyes narrowed and his gaze flitted back and forth between them.

Holy what? Violet's mouth fell open. *Surely she'd misheard.* She turned to Emmett, and the expression on his face told her she hadn't. Her mouth went dry and she tried to swallow the burgeoning knot in her throat.

"I'm not sure what you've been told," Emmett said, "but..."

Pastor Collins raised his hand. "The message has been sent down from Almighty God himself," he closed his eyes and shook his head, raising both hands in the air.

"What message is that?" Emmett challenged.

The preacher's eyes snapped open and he fixed Emmett with a piercing glare. "[*T*]*he wife of the dead shall not marry without unto a stranger: her husband's brother shall go in unto her, and take her to him to wife, and perform the duty of an husband's brother unto her,"* he said loudly, his voice shaking with emotion.

Several people turned to stare at them, and Violet's face grew hot. "Surely you don't expect . . ."

"The Good Book commands it," Pastor Collins bellowed.

"Pastor Collins! Pastor Collins!" an out-of-breath voice called from down the street.

Violet turned and saw Peggy Blanchard running towards them, one hand holding up her skirt and the other waving in the air to draw their attention.

"Come quickly," Peggy called, her breath coming in ragged gasps. "It's Mrs. Froman."

Pastor Collins's thin lips pressed into an even thinner line and he turned to Emmett. "I'll be expecting you," he said, then turned on his heel and hurried in the other direction with Mrs. Blanchard.

Violet stared at the spot where Pastor Collins had just been, and her face burned as though it was on fire. She couldn't bring herself to look at Emmett. The pastor couldn't force them to marry, could he? No, that wasn't possible. Emmett had a job to return to in Denver, he couldn't stay here. Despite the attention he'd showered on her earlier, Violet wasn't naive enough to believe he wanted to marry her. How had this wonderful, perfect day turned sour so quickly?

She worried her bottom lip with her teeth and thought about the other couples in town that had recently been married. What would happen if they just refused and Emmett left? Could the pastor make her leave Last Chance? Did he have the authority to do such a thing?

A heaviness settled in her chest and her grip on Emmett's arm tightened. She struggled to catch her breath as tears burned the back of her eyes. She couldn't return to Charleston. Where would she go? What would she do?

"Here, take a sip of this," Emmett said in a low, gentle voice. Violet felt his large hand close over hers and guide the bottle of Sarsaparilla up to her mouth. She took a couple of long swallows of the cool liquid, followed by several deep breaths.

"Pay him no mind," Emmett said.

"But..."

Emmett turned to face her and looked deep into her eyes. "There is no need for concern," he said softly. "I'll come back tomorrow and talk to him."

She tilted her head back and a strange calmness came over her as she stared back at him. His gaze softened and shifted from her eyes to her mouth and back. Her heart raced and her throat went dry, making it impossible for her to speak. Was he going to kiss her? Out here in the middle of the street?

"Violet, I was hoping to catch you," a woman's voice came from behind her.

Violet jumped, startled by the sound of someone calling her name. Emmett took a step back, and Violet spun around to see who it was. Faith Thornton approached her, waving an envelope in the air. Violet's stomach clenched with an odd mix of disappointment and curiosity. She glanced back at Emmett for just a moment before turning to greet the woman who now stood next to them.

"Hi Faith," she said. Faith's husband, Aaron, was also killed in the blizzard. Cora had told Violet what an awful time Faith had had recovering, but there was a new man in town named Beau that had taken an interest in Faith. Violet took in Faith's carefully styled hair and neatly pressed dress, along with the flush of color on her cheeks and hoped it was true.

"I'm sorry to uh, interrupt." Faith threw a quick glance at Emmett and gave Violet a timid smile. "This telegram came for you earlier this week," she held the envelope toward Violet. "I saw you through the window and thought I'd bring it out."

Violet's eyes grew wide and her breath caught in her throat. *Who would send her a telegram?* The only person that truly knew she was there was her father's attorney, and he had no reason to contact her. She stared at the envelope but was unable to make herself reach for it. Faith frowned and held the envelope closer. Violet took an involuntary step back and clutched the skirt of her gown with trembling fingers.

"Thank you, Faith, that was very thoughtful of you," Emmett said, and reached for the envelope.

Faith hesitated for a brief moment, then placed it in his outstretched hand. She cast a concerned look at Violet, then gave an awkward little wave. "I best be getting back," she said, and turned and hurried back toward the Post Office.

Violet stood frozen, unable to move, hardly daring to breathe. She scrunched her eyes shut and thought maybe if she didn't look at it, it would disappear and she would discover that this had merely been some sort of strange hallucination brought on by the Sarsaparilla.

"Violet?"

Emmett's deep voice made her stomach quiver and she opened her eyes just enough to see the envelope still grasped between his fingers. Something her father used to say when she was young popped into her head. *You cannot escape the responsibility of tomorrow by evading it today.*

Violet took a deep, shaking breath and opened her eyes. Without a word, she took the envelope out of Emmett's hand and ran her finger under the flap. Inside was a single piece of paper. She could scarcely breathe as she unfolded and read it.

Mrs. Violet Stapleton, Last Chance, Nebraska.

Reason to suspect Dorcas Montgomery en route to Last Chance. Use caution.

~ Bartholomew Vesprey, Attorney at Law

Violet's blood ran cold as the implication of the words hit her. The bottle of Sarsaparilla slid from her fingers and landed with a dull thud on the sidewalk, spilling what remained of its contents. *If Faith received the telegram earlier in the week, was it possible Aunt Dorcas was already in Last Chance?* Her eyes darted up and down the street for any sign of her.

"Violet, what is it?"

She turned to Emmett but unable to hold his gaze, she looked away. *Could she trust him? Did she want to involve him? Or Cora? What if they got hurt?* She couldn't risk it.

"I don't wish to discuss it. Please take me home," she said stiffly, willing herself to hold her tears at bay.

A line etched between his brows as he studied her for a moment. He opened his mouth but she lifted her hand to stop him.

"Please, Emmett. Just take me home."

Chapter Seven

♥

They rode back to the farm in uncomfortable silence. Emmett tried to engage Violet in conversation a couple of times, but she stared straight ahead, lost in her thoughts. He wished she would have shared what was in the telegram, but it was very clear to him that she meant to keep it to herself.

While Violet had told him many things about what Charleston was like, she had shared very little about her life there. He still didn't know exactly what it was that had brought her to Last Chance, and once again began to wonder if she was hiding something.

Emmett brought the buggy to a stop in front of the house and went around the other side to help Violet down. She murmured her thanks, but avoided eye contact with him and hurried into the house, shutting the door behind her without a backward glance.

He stared at the closed door for a long moment, wondering what he should do. He spent countless hours over the last decade with Mr. Hanna learning to be a confident businessman, but when it came to women, Emmett was very unsure of himself. One thing he was certain of though, Violet had captivated him in a way no one else ever had.

Emmett let out a long breath and proceeded to the barn. There he unhitched the buggy, fed, watered the horse, and put him in his stall. A scraping sound at the other end of the barn drew his attention and he went over to investigate.

Eli stood at the workbench with his back to Emmett and appeared to be sanding the outside of a wooden box. The box was skillfully crafted with complex dovetail joints and a hinged lid.

Emmett watched him work for several minutes in wonder. How did he not know about his brother's talent? Had he been so self-absorbed in the weeks he'd been back at the farm that he had paid so little attention to him? His stomach sank as he realized how little he really knew about his only remaining brother.

Eli must have sensed his presence because his hand stilled and he turned his head and glanced at Emmett over his shoulder. His shoulders stiffened and he narrowed his eyes. "What do you want?"

Emmett blinked back at his younger brother and found himself at a loss for words. Suddenly he remembered the bottle of Sarsaparilla in his pocket. He made a mental note to thank Violet later for her insight, then removed it and held it out toward Eli. "I brought you some Sarsaparilla. I thought you might like it."

Eli's eyes grew wide and a smile began to form on his lips, but then it disappeared, as quickly as it had come and he turned back to the bench. "I don't need anything from you."

Emmett stiffened and felt his jaw tighten, but that feeling was quickly replaced with the sting of disappointment. He let his chin drop to his chest and closed his eyes. What kind of example was he for his brother?

He thought about what his mother said and knew it would be up to him to mend the fence between him and Eli. She was right, Eli had practically been a baby when he left. He'd given no thought to how that might affect him, nor had he thought about the burden he'd inadvertently placed on Eli when he hadn't returned immediately after Wyatt's death.

Emmett stepped forward and placed the bottle on the bench next to Eli. "Violet asked me to buy it for you," he said.

Eli looked up and raised an eyebrow. "Violet?"

Emmett nodded. "We were in town and I wanted to . . .," he hesitated, then decided to confide in him, "impress her."

Eli snorted and lifted the bottle. "You wanted to impress her. By buying her a Sarsaparilla?" He opened the bottle, glanced at Emmett, and let out a little laugh before taking a long drink.

Emmett rubbed his forehead as he thought about how absurd that sounded. He wondered if Violet thought so too. Who tried to impress a woman with a bottle of Sarsaparilla? He should have consulted . . . he mentally went through a list of the names of the people he knew in Last Chance, but no one he could have asked came to mind. He clenched his jaw. Well, he should have asked someone for advice before making such a foolish decision.

Eli lowered the bottle and his expression softened. "You were serious, weren't you?"

Heat flooded Emmett's cheeks, and he pursed his lips and looked away. He should have known better. He was scheduled to return to Denver very soon, he never should have asked her to accompany him to town. What had he been thinking? He squared his shoulders and picked some invisible lint from the sleeve of his frock coat.

"Yes, well, it doesn't matter," he said, trying his best to sound indifferent. His gaze traveled to the box Eli was working on and he pointed to it. "What have you got there?"

Eli studied him thoughtfully for a moment, then set down the bottle and lifted up the box. He held it out to Emmett, who took it and examined it closely. It was a fairly simple box, but the workmanship on it was exquisite and he could tell a great deal of care had been taken while making it.

"It's a flour bin," Eli explained, and lifted the lid to expose two compartments. "I saw one like it in Mrs. Parker's kitchen." Now it was his turn to look away, as his cheeks tinged a bright shade of pink. "I thought maybe Ma would like it for her birthday."

A lump formed in the back of Emmett's throat. He was touched by the thoughtfulness of the gesture, and realized there was much more to his little brother than he'd thought. It also reminded him that he'd nearly forgotten about their mother's birthday.

"That's a fine gift," he said. "I'm sure she'll love it." He handed the box back to Eli and raised an eyebrow. "Who is Mrs. Parker?"

Eli carefully placed the box back on the workbench and lifted the bottle of Sarsaparilla to his lips, taking another long drink before he answered. "She used to be Mrs. Fulton, I didn't know her before, but then Cullen, I mean Mr. Parker, came to town and married her. He runs the sawmill."

Emmett frowned. "I thought Mr. Hensel ran the sawmill."

"He did, but then . . . well, you know, the blizzard came."

Emmett nodded. The town had changed so much since he'd last been home.

Eli finished the rest of the liquid in the bottle and let out a long belch, then covered his mouth with his hand. Emmett wasn't sure if he was trying to cover up his ill manners or suppress laughter. He reminded himself that at age fifteen, Eli was still a boy and boys will be boys.

"Mr. Parker showed me how to make it," Eli gestured at the box. "Sometimes I help him and Ben, and then he'll show me how to make things."

"Ben?"

"Mr. Parker's brother. He lives in Mrs. Parker's old house."

"Does he work at the mill too?"

Eli pressed his lips together in a frown. "No," he hedged. "Ma says he's a simple man. He mostly stays at his farm. He doesn't say much."

Emmett's gaze roamed over the workbench, and he noticed for the first time several different tools than his father had had. Based on the amount of sawdust and wood shavings scattered about, the boy spent quite a bit of time here.

"You did a fine job on that box," he said.

Eli's eyes widened and a bright smile filled his face. "Do you really think so?" he asked.

Emmett returned the smile and nodded. "I do. You enjoy woodworking?"

"Yes, Mr. Parker said he'd teach me how to carve too. When I have time. There's a lot of stuff to do here, so I don't get to go over there very often."

Emmett felt his shoulders slump, even though Eli's tone hadn't been accusatory. He'd been so focused on his own career, he hadn't even considered that his brother might have other ambitions besides working the farm. He'd always assumed that Eli's interests were the same as Wyatt's.

"Ma said you've done a fine job keeping things up here since . . ." Emmett trailed off.

Eli's chin dropped and he nodded. "I'm trying," he said. "I know I don't do things the same as Wyatt did."

"Wyatt had his own way of doing things."

Eli looked up and a crease formed between his brows. "I have ideas too," he said. "I been talking to Mr. Pete." When Emmett frowned, Eli explained. "Mr. Pete is the president of the Grange."

"What kind of ideas?" Emmett was curious. The bank he worked at in Denver had given out more farm loans in recent years primarily due to influence from the Grange.

Eli twisted his mouth and toed the dirt floor with his shoe for a moment before he responded. "Mr. Pete said there's more money in planting corn than wheat, and the soil here is good for corn. But it's more work too."

Emmett raised his brows. When he was fifteen, the last thing on his mind was the best type of crop to plant. But then, his nose had always been stuck in a book. He also didn't have the responsibility on his shoulders that Eli did. He may have been the oldest, but his father had still been around then. And his brothers. Now, he was the only brother Eli had left and Eli was right, he'd abandoned him.

He rubbed the back of his neck and closed his eyes for a moment. An idea began to form in his mind. When he went back into town, he'd make some inquiries. If things checked out, he'd make a call on Ben Parker. Maybe he could make things right. He wouldn't say anything yet, though. Not until he knew for certain.

Emmett took a step closer and hesitated for a moment before placing a hand on Eli's shoulder. "You're turning into a fine man," he gave Eli's shoulder a light squeeze, then stepped back. "I'm sorry I didn't come home sooner."

Eli blinked back at him, and was quiet for a long moment. He shuffled his feet, then said, "I'm sorry I hit you."

Emmett let out a small laugh. "It's all right, I deserved it."

Eli grinned. "I never said you didn't deserve it."

They laughed and Emmett pulled his watch out of his pocket and glanced at it. "I need to change out of these clothes, then I'll come back to help with the chores." He turned to leave.

"I'll do chores tonight," Eli called from behind him. "You don't need to come back out."

Emmett hesitated and looked back.

"It's no problem," Eli said with a smile, and shrugged his thin shoulders. "What are brothers for?"

A lightness came over Emmett. He felt cleared of an enormous load of guilt he hadn't been entirely aware he'd been carrying. "Thank you," he said, and gave Eli a grateful smile and pulled the door open.

"I think she likes you."

Emmett froze, mid-step. He glanced over his shoulder at Eli and frowned.

"Violet," Eli grinned. "I think she likes you."

Emmett pondered Eli's words as he walked across the yard toward the house. *Was it possible?* He could all but hear Mr. Hanna's diatribe about women being an unnecessary distraction. He had readily agreed with him at the time, but now, Emmett wasn't so sure his mentor was right.

He stepped into the house and looked around. His mother was in the kitchen, kneading dough, but Violet was nowhere to be seen.

"She's in her room," his mother said, glancing at the closed door of Violet's bedroom. "She was quite upset when she came in. What happened?"

Emmett slipped out of his frock coat and hung it on a peg, then crossed the room and took a seat at the table where his mother worked and ran his hands through his hair.

He told her about their encounter with Pastor Collins and the mysterious telegram Faith had given Violet.

"Pastor Collins is a piece of work," she said, and flipped the dough over, kneading it a little harder than she had on the other side. "But it's wrong to speak ill of a man of the cloth." She gave Emmett a look that indicated she had plenty to say on the matter, but her sense of decorum wouldn't allow it. "Violet didn't say who the telegram was from?"

Emmett shook his head and reached his hand out, pinched off a tiny piece of dough, and popped it in his mouth. His mother swatted at his hand and narrowed her eyes at him.

"That's enough of that. I would have thought you'd have outgrown such mischief by now." The tone of her voice was sharp, but the sparkle in her eyes told him she wasn't really upset with him.

He shrugged and gave her a sheepish grin. Emmett missed moments like this. His thoughts strayed for an instant to the latest message from

Mr. Hanna, but he pushed them from his mind. He didn't want to think about Denver right now. He slid a quick glance to Violet's closed door and wondered what she was doing.

He looked back at his mother to find her watching him intently. "I want to show you something," she said. "Let me just get this finished."

She lifted the dough into a bowl and covered it with a clean towel. Then she washed her hands and dried them on her apron.

"Come with me," she said, and beckoned for him to follow her into her bedroom.

The room looked just as it had the last time he'd been in it, just after his father's funeral. A small, framed photograph of his parents still stood on the dresser next to his father's razor and shaving brush. Emmett's stomach rolled as he thought of everything his mother had been through. She'd buried her husband and two of her children. And all he could think about was getting promoted at work. He hung his head in shame.

"Emmett? What's wrong?"

His mother touched his arm, but he couldn't bring himself to look at her.

"I'm sorry," he said, trying to keep his voice from wavering. "I should have stayed here after Father and William were killed." He shook his head. "No, I never should have left in the first place. Wyatt was right . . ."

"Stop right there," his mother interrupted him. "You can't alter what is in the past, so there's no sense in trying. You don't know that staying here would have changed anything. God called them home when He saw fit. It's not our place to judge that timing, even when we don't understand it."

"But if . . ."

"But nothing." She let out a long sigh and sat on the edge of the bed. She grasped Emmett's hand and pulled him down beside her. "You and Wyatt," she continued, "I've never seen two brothers that were more different. If you said something was red, he'd say it was blue just to spite you. The two of you were like oil and water. Always rubbing each other the wrong way."

Emmett stared at the floor. She was right. They constantly bickered with each other. Foolish, petty arguments that meant nothing now.

"After the accident, Wyatt was consumed with grief and anger. He lashed out at you because it was the easiest thing for him to do. I know he was sorry afterward," she said. "But by then he didn't know how to apologize."

Emmett understood that all too well. He'd been just seventeen years old when he left home. His dreams were bigger than what he could find in the small town of Last Chance. He'd had words with his father, they'd both said some awful things, and he'd left. After some time had passed he wanted to make amends, but didn't know how either. Now it was too late.

"I shouldn't have left."

"You had different dreams than your father and your brothers. You needed to leave in order to follow those dreams. There is nothing wrong with that, Emmett."

"But I should have been here for you. For Eli."

"You're here now." She smiled and gave his hand a gentle squeeze.

For the second time that day, Emmett felt as though a weight had been lifted from his shoulders.

"So, tell me about Violet."

His left eyebrow shot up. "What about her?"

"Emmett," she said softly, and gave him a knowing smile. "I've seen how you look at her."

Emmett averted his gaze as heat rushed to his face. *Was he that transparent? Was it so obvious to Violet as well?* This wasn't part of his plan. His plan had been to come home, help get the crop planted and get back to Denver as quickly as possible. He rubbed his hand over his face and sighed heavily.

"She's nothing like I expected," he said.

"What do you mean?"

Emmett sat for a minute and contemplated how to explain something he didn't fully understand himself. "It surprised me that Wyatt would have chosen someone so . . . refined to marry."

"You don't think she fits well on the farm?"

He raised his eyebrows. "Do you?"

"She tries."

"She does," he conceded. "I guess I would have thought Wyatt would have chosen someone local, not someone with such a bourgeois background. He was . . . Wyatt was like a tin of water. Violet is whiskey in a teacup."

A smile teased the corners of his mother's mouth. She stood and walked across the room, stopping in front of an old trunk nestled in the corner. She knelt on the floor in front of it and lifted the lid. The trunk had been there as long as Emmett could remember, but he'd never looked inside. He rose and crossed the room to get a better look.

She pulled out a white satin gown and gently, almost reverently, spread it across her lap. It looked like something Violet might wear. She ran her fingers down the front of the dress and gazed wistfully at it for a moment before reaching back into the trunk. She brought out a pair of white kid gloves and an ostrich feather fan.

He watched in amazement as she spread the fan open, and fluttered it close to her face, her eyes sparkling at him over the feathered edge.

"I wore this at my debutante ball," she smiled at him, a faraway look in her eyes.

Emmett blinked at her incredulously. *His mother was a debutante? How did he not know this?* He knew she'd come from out east, but she didn't speak about her family, and he'd never asked. His brows knitted together as he took in her worn grey calico dress and plain white apron, then slid his gaze back to the ball gown and tried to imagine what she looked like wearing it.

"You look surprised."

He nodded. "It's a beautiful gown."

"Thank you." She rooted in the trunk for a moment longer, removed a small box and regarded it carefully before she slipped it into her apron pocket. Then she placed the dress, gloves and fan back in the trunk. She let her fingers slide across the satin fabric of the gown one last time and closed the lid.

Emmett extended a hand and helped her to her feet. His mind was filled with questions about the woman that stood in front of him. He had always only looked at her as his mother, not as a woman who'd attended debutante balls.

"My family was not so very different from Violet's," his mother said, and walked over to the window. She pulled aside the curtain and peered through the glass, staring off into the distance.

"My father was a manager at the Boston Manufacturing Company. We had a fine house and Mother did a lot of entertaining, including my debutante ball. She had high hopes of finding me an aristocratic husband."

Emmett leaned against the dresser and listened to her speak with rapt attention. *How did a Boston blue-blood end up on a farm in Nebraska?*

"But I had been reading about the expansion west," she continued, "and when Father suggested I go to Wheaton, I demurred. My dear friend, Ordelyea suggested we reply to matrimonial advertisements, and that's how I met your father."

"You were a mail order bride? But I thought you loved Father."

His mother turned away from the window and looked at him, her eyes brimming with tears. "Oh Emmett, I did love your father. I loved him more than I thought I could ever love a man."

Emmett pulled a handkerchief from his pocket and handed it to her as he pondered her words.

She gave him a small, grateful smile and dabbed her eyes dry.

"When I came to Last Chance, I didn't fit in very well either. Your father's family took me in and became my family." She fixed him with a pointed stare. "Now do you see why I had to let Violet stay? She needs us."

As he stared back at his mother, Emmett's chest swelled. In the years he'd been away, it was easy to forget how important family was. Maybe she was right, maybe Violet did need them. He just wished he knew what it was she was hiding.

"What will you tell Pastor Collins?"

Emmett ran his fingers through his hair and let out a breath of frustration. He saw how the preacher's threat affected Violet, but they hadn't had a chance to discuss it because of the telegram. She'd refused to speak about any of it on the drive back from town.

"I don't know," he replied. "Mr. Hanna has been more than patient with my absence. It was rather presumptuous of the pastor to assume that's why I returned to Last Chance. My job is in Denver," he said, but even he could hear the lack of conviction in his own voice.

"What if you took her back to Denver with you?" his mother suggested with a hopeful smile.

Emmett would be lying if he said the thought hadn't crossed his mind. He was still trying to formulate a response when she reached into her apron pocket, pulled out the small leather box she'd removed from the trunk and handed it to him.

"This belonged to my mother," she said.

He swallowed hard, his throat suddenly dry. The box was old and the leather was cracked in several places. He gingerly lifted the lid and stared at the glittering ring nestled inside. A large amethyst, surrounded by small pearls, was set in the middle of an ornately carved gold band. Emmett found himself imagining what the stunning piece of jewelry would look like on Violet's finger.

His stomach twisted into knots and his heart grew heavy as he recalled the conversation he'd had with his mother right after he'd come home from Denver where she'd told him Violet was the daughter she'd never had. If he took her to Denver, and that was even assuming she'd want to go, he'd be taking her away from his mother. She'd had enough loss in her life.

Emmett snapped the lid closed and handed the box back to his mother. "I can't," he said, his voice thick with emotion, unable to meet her eyes.

"Can't or won't?"

Emmett squeezed his eyes shut and turned away. *What was the difference?* "She came here to be with Wyatt, not me."

She put her hand on his arm, but he pulled it away and turned to face her. For a second his throat grew tight and he took a deep breath to steady his voice.

"What would people think? That I'm marrying her out of pity? Out of duty?"

"You care so much about what other people think that you'd throw away a chance at happiness? A chance at love?"

"Love?" he chuffed. "What's love got to do with it?"

"I've seen the way you two look at each other. Who cares what it looks like? Time will prove otherwise."

He shook his head vehemently. "It's not possible."

His mother gave him a knowing smile. "It doesn't always take a long courtship to fall in love with someone, Emmett."

Love? Could it be? No. They hadn't even known each other for two months. *The idea was preposterous, wasn't it?* His mind raced as he thought about the possible consequences of marrying her so soon, both socially and to his family.

"I'm sorry, Mother," he said, "I can't." And walked out of the room.

Chapter Eight

♥

The next several days on the farm were quiet. Almost too quiet. Cora had asked Violet to join her for a trip into town early that morning but Violet declined, complaining of a headache. It pained her, to be dishonest, but if her Aunt Dorcas was really coming to Last Chance, she couldn't risk running into her.

Her stomach rolled at the thought of what would happen if Aunt Dorcas found her. Mr. Vesprey was quite clear that she was not to be trusted, and although Violet already knew that, having it reiterated to her by someone in his profession sent chills down her spine.

Her first impulse had been to run. But she didn't know where to go. Sure, she had the means, but how would she explain it to Cora? Even if she did leave, she was now certain that it would only be a matter of time until her Aunt found her again. No, staying put was the best thing she could do for now. Maybe she wouldn't need to worry about it. Maybe the attorney was wrong.

Violet wished she could talk to someone about the situation. She missed her best friend, Annabelle. She hadn't had any contact with her since she'd arrived in Last Chance. Annabelle would be the first person Aunt Dorcas would run to, and Violet didn't want to put her in a position where she'd have to lie. So, the two of them had decided Annabelle couldn't know where Violet was either.

Violet hadn't had the opportunity since she came to Last Chance to make any real friends.

She'd met several women that seemed really nice, but living out on the farm made it hard and Violet wasn't sure who she could trust. Several times she nearly broke down and told Cora everything, but Aunt Dorcas's words kept running through her head: *Who will believe you over me?*

Violet sat with Daisy and stared out the window. It had rained during the night, and the ground was still wet and dotted with puddles here and there. Tears blurred her vision as she pulled Daisy close for a hug. She didn't know what she'd do without the little dog.

Emmett had been avoiding her since their ill-fated trip into town. Thankfully, he hadn't inquired further about the telegram she'd received, and Cora seemed none the wiser about it. She detected some tension between Cora and Emmett that hadn't been there before though, and wondered what had transpired between them.

Violet caught Emmett staring at her several times like he wanted to say something, but he always looked away as soon as their eyes met. As she brushed Daisy, she thought about the moment her and Emmett had shared outside the mercantile. Perhaps he hadn't been about to kiss her after all. Was it possible she'd imagined the whole thing?

She was still pondering that question when the buggy rolled into the yard. Violet wiped the tears from her eyes and cheeks as she watched Eli rush out of the barn to help Cora down and then lead the horse through the large, open barn doors. Cora carried several small, paper wrapped packages and one much larger one toward the house. A happy smile lit up her face, and Violet wished she could have gone with her.

Cora stepped into the house and her eyebrows rose when her gaze landed on Violet and Daisy.

"Violet, are you feeling better?" she asked, her voice full of concern. "Your eyes are a bit red.

Perhaps you should lay back down?"

"I'm feeling much better, thank you," she said through a tight throat. Guilt over the lie she'd told coursed through her veins. She turned her head to hide the quiver in her lip, and tried to blink back a fresh wave of tears. Her parents would be so disappointed in her.

"Good, I'm happy to hear that." Cora crossed the room and placed her packages on the table. "Would you join me for some tea? Phyllis ordered a new blend she thought you might enjoy and she sent it home with me, along with her well wishes."

Violet stared at Daisy for a moment before responding. *Phyllis Talley thought to order tea for her?* The little dog looked up at her and stared at her intently, as if trying to let her know she wasn't as alone as she felt. She swiped under her eyes with her fingers and planted a kiss on top of Daisy's head before setting her on the floor. She rose, turned to Cora and smiled her first genuine smile in days.

"That was very kind of her. Tea sounds wonderful, thank you."

Cora returned her smile and set about measuring out the tea leaves into the teapot just as Violet had taught her. She poured hot water from the kettle on the stove into the teapot to let the leaves steep. Violet took two tea cups out of the cupboard, along with the small bowl of sugar, then pulled the jar of milk out from under the sink and set them on the table before taking a seat.

"Phyllis said it's called Earl Grey," Cora said, and poured hot tea into their cups. "It's such a strange name for a tea." She placed a cup in front of Violet and sat in the chair across from her.

Violet nodded in agreement, lifted the cup and inhaled the familiar scent of black tea. Mingled in with the sweet, slightly floral aroma were notes of bitter orange. She took a tentative sip. The tea was rich and bold with distinct hints of citrus.

"It's unusual, but quite good," she said, carefully setting her cup in front of her. She liked the unexpected sweet yet tart flavor of the tea and made a mental note to thank Phyllis next time she was in town. Her smile faltered for just a moment as she thought about going to town again. When would it be safe, and how would she know?

"It's definitely interesting," Cora said, trying to hold back a grin. She gave a noncommittal shrug. "As much as I want to like tea, I think I may always prefer coffee."

"My father preferred coffee over tea as well."

"And your mother?"

"She loved tea and insisted on hosting regular afternoon tea parties." Violet drew her eyebrows together and stared into her cup. She had always loved it when her mother hosted tea because their cook would make the most amazing little sandwiches and cakes.

"You must miss that," Cora said, and gave her a sympathetic smile.

"I do, very much."

They sat for a moment in silence. Then Cora reached for the larger of the packages she'd brought from town, untied the string and unfolded the paper wrap. Inside lay several yards of navy calico dotted with tiny white flowers.

"The mercantile got in some new fabric. I found a lovely pattern for a dress in one of the Godey's Lady's Books you lent me, and thought this material would be perfect for it." She gently ran the tips of her fingers over the cloth as though she'd never seen anything so fine.

Maybe she hadn't. Nearly all of Cora's dresses were neutral in color, even her Sunday best dress was brown.

"It's beautiful," Violet said. "That color will look lovely on you. I'm glad you were able to find the books of some use." Aunt Dorcas had insisted she subscribe to Godey's to keep up with the latest fashions, but Violet liked reading the articles and stories in each issue. She was happy she'd brought them with her, as she'd reread many of them over the long winter months.

"Actually, I was hoping you might help me with the dress."

Violet's eyes lit up and she started to smile, but quickly remembered she didn't have the proper skills for such an undertaking. Mending was one thing, but piecing and sewing a whole dress was an entirely different matter. It was just one more item to add to the already very long list of things she didn't know how to do. *Maybe her Aunt Dorcas was right, maybe she was worthless.*

"I couldn't possibly," she said, her eyes downcast. "I've never sewn a dress. I couldn't bear it if I ruined it."

"I've seen your needlework, it will be just fine. We can work on it together."

Violet lifted her gaze and gave a tentative smile. "Thank you, Cora. I'll be happy to help."

"You'll be doing me the favor. We can start after dinner," Cora replied, rubbing the swollen joints on her fingers. She unwrapped the other two packages, the first of which contained navy thread and buttons. The second contained a length of satin navy blue ribbon and Cora laid it across the calico.

"Oh Cora, that matches perfectly."

"It does, doesn't it?" She stared at the fabric on the table for a moment, then looked back at Violet and gave her a warm smile. "Working together will make it more enjoyable too."

Violet tried to swallow down the lump that formed in the back of her throat. This woman, who wasn't even a blood relative, had shown her more kindness in the months she'd been there than her Aunt had in all the years she'd lived with her.

"Thank you, Cora," she said, her voice barely above a whisper.

Cora's brows drew together in question.

"For letting me stay here." She lowered her gaze and the teacup swam in front of her eyes.

Cora reached across the table and squeezed her hand. "You are exactly where you are meant to be. God has every moment of our lives planned for us from the moment we are born. He knows when you wake and when you sleep. He knows the words you will say before you speak them. God brought you to us for a reason." She patted Violet's hand, then straightened in her chair.

"But Wyatt . . . we didn't even . . . he was gone so suddenly." Heat flushed her cheeks and she hoped Cora didn't notice.

"Perhaps Wyatt was only part of the reason you're here."

Violet frowned. "I'm not sure I understand."

Before Cora had a chance to answer, Violet heard the clip-clop of an approaching horse and buggy. Cora turned toward the window and frowned.

"I wonder who that could be. I hope it's not Pastor Collins," she said as she rose and walked toward the door.

Violet froze. Her hands began to tremble and she closed her eyes and prayed. *Please God, don't let it be Aunt Dorcas.* She heard the click of the door and felt the whisper of a cool breeze as Cora pulled the door open.

Please don't let it be Aunt Dorcas. Violet held her breath, not even daring to breathe as she waited to find out who it was. Right now, she'd be ecstatic if it turned out to be Pastor Collins.

Daisy began to bark furiously and Violet's eyes flew open as she realized the door was still ajar. The little white dog slipped past Cora and ran out into the yard.

"Daisy, stop!" She jumped from her chair and bolted toward the door. The horse and buggy were nearly at the house when Violet spotted Daisy. Right under the horse's legs. Violet's heart hammered in her chest and her breath caught in her throat. The buggy rolled to a stop next to the house, but there was no sign of Daisy.

Violet ran toward the buggy, not even caring to look who was inside. She didn't know what she would do if something happened to her precious dog. She stooped next to the back wheel, cringing as she looked underneath, but Daisy wasn't there. That's when she heard Cora's sharp intake of breath behind her. She turned to see Cora standing with her hand over her mouth, her gaze fixed on the ground behind the buggy.

Violet held her breath as she turned to look where Cora was staring. A white fluff of fur lay still on the muddy ground, and a sick wave of recognition washed over her. It was Daisy.

"No! Daisy No!" Violet let out a strangled cry and ran toward the dog. She dropped to her knees in front of the motionless animal, heedless of the mud soaking through her dress. Tears blurred her vision and she was unable to tell if Daisy was breathing or not. She vaguely heard Cora calling for Emmett, then footsteps running toward her.

"What happened?" Emmett asked, kneeling beside her.

"I - I don't know," Violet choked out. "She slipped out the door and the horse was on top of her . . . and I don't know if she's . . ." Her words were cut off by a sob and she brought her hand up to cover her mouth.

"I'm sorry," a male voice said, and a man crouched down beside Emmett. Violet glanced up and recognized Dave McFarland from the livery.

"I didn't see it until it was already under the buggy," Dave said, removing his hat. He ran a hand through his hair and replaced the hat. "Is . . . is that a dog?"

Violet glared at him. "Of course it's a dog," she snapped, then instantly regretted her sharp tongue. She softened her gaze. "That's my Daisy," she turned back to Emmett. "Is she . . ." she trailed off, unable to say the word.

Emmett placed his hand on the dog's side and held it there for a moment. "She's breathing," he said, and Violet swallowed a sigh of relief.

"Of course she is," an all too familiar voice said from behind her. "That . . . mongrel has more lives than a cat."

Aunt Dorcas. The sound of her voice sent a wave of nausea through Violet's already knotted stomach. She closed her eyes for a moment and tried to steady her nerves. Violet slowly lifted her head and met Aunt Dorcas's cold stare. She looked exactly as expected in her usual dark dress and white lace cap over dark hair that was now streaked with grey. Her lips were pursed in a permanent expression of disdain. Goose-flesh sprang up on Violet's neck as a cold shiver ran through her body.

Behind her Aunt, Violet could see Eli running toward them. He gave Aunt Dorcas a curious glance, then turned to Emmett.

"What happened?" he asked his brother.

"She went under the buggy. I don't know how injured she is, but she's alive."

"Do you want me to get Dr. Spaulding?" Dave asked.

Emmett lifted his head and gave him a questioning look. "Who is that? Why would we call the doctor?"

"He's staying in the back room at the livery. Came from the east. He treats animals as well and might be able to help the pup."

"Yes, please," Violet pleaded. She'd do anything to save Daisy.

"I'll go," Eli said. "My horse will be faster without the buggy behind it." He whirled around and ran toward the barn. Moments later, he emerged on the back of his horse heading toward town at a full gallop.

"Let's get her inside," Emmett said, and carefully lifted the little dog. She was completely limp and her head lolled to the side like a broken doll, the tip of her pink tongue barely visible through a tangle of dirty white fur.

Cora appeared and handed Emmett a towel. He gingerly wrapped it around Daisy, then stood.

Violet pressed her fist against her mouth and tried to retain a modicum of self-control. Tears streamed down her cheeks and a sob broke from her chest.

Cora helped her to her feet, put a comforting arm around her shoulders and gave her a reassuring squeeze.

"Oh for pity's sake," Aunt Dorcas said with a roll of her eyes. "Must you always be so melodramatic?"

Emmett glared at the woman, then slid an irritated glance at Dave. "Who is this? And what is she doing here?"

Before Dave could respond, Aunt Dorcas stepped forward. She lifted her chin and met Emmett's gaze square-on.

"I am Dorcas Montgomery," she said haughtily. "I'm Violet's aunt. I've come to return her to

Charleston so she can face charges of theft and attempted murder."

Chapter Nine

♥

*A*ttempted murder? Violet? Emmett was so stunned he nearly lost his grip on Daisy. He'd always had a hunch Violet was hiding something, but would have never guessed anything so heinous. *It made no sense. There had to be some logical explanation.*

His mother and Dave stood and stared at Dorcas with their mouths open, but Emmett turned to look at Violet. The color had drained from her face, and she'd taken on a dazed and chalky look. He was grateful his mother still had an arm around her because she didn't look very steady on her feet.

"Let's go inside and sort this out," he said, anxious to get to the bottom of things.

"Good idea," his mother said, giving him a concerned look. "I'll put on a fresh pot of coffee."

"Hmmph," Dorcas sniffed and mumbled something under her breath before she followed his mother inside.

Dave hesitated. "Uh, I think I'll head back to the livery," he said, toeing the dirt with his boot. "This seems like a family matter."

"Would you mind waiting for a few minutes? I have a feeling Violet's aunt will not be here overly long." *Not if he could help it, anyways.* He couldn't remember ever having a stronger dislike for someone he'd only just met.

"I can wait for a short while," Dave agreed, looking relieved.

Emmett didn't blame him for wanting to avoid the conversation that was about to take place. He nodded his appreciation, took a deep breath and went inside.

Dorcas stood just inside the door forcing him to step around her. His mother had made up a pallet on the floor with a couple of blankets for Daisy and beckoned him over. Violet stood near her as though she were frozen. He'd never seen her look that way before and wasn't sure if the expression on her face was guilt, fear or a mixture of both.

Emmett gently laid the small dog, still wrapped in the towel, on the makeshift bed, and held his hand against her chest again to make sure she was still breathing. He let out a small sigh of relief when he felt movement, and prayed Eli would hurry back with Dr. Spaulding.

His mother rose and started toward the kitchen.

Emmett's gaze flitted between Violet and her aunt. Aside from the same dark color of hair, there was very little familial resemblance. Her aunt was much taller than Violet, and held herself with an air of power and authority that told Emmett she was used to getting her way. He'd dealt with many customers at the bank in Denver that had the same sense of self-importance and was not intimidated by her. He walked to the table, pulled out a chair and gave Dorcas a pointed look. "Have a seat so we can discuss this."

Dorcas stiffened and lifted her chin. "I'll not be told what to do by a . . . ," she glanced around the room with disdain, "simple farmer." Her gaze landed on Violet. "Don't you think you ought to change out of that dress you've ruined, crawling around in the mud like a -"

"That's enough!" Emmett spat the words through gritted teeth. "You can leave right now or you can sit and explain yourself."

Dorcas's nostrils flared and her eyes narrowed as she glared at him, but she closed her mouth and strode to the table. She pulled a lace trimmed handkerchief from her reticule and wiped off the chair before taking her seat.

Emmett turned to Violet, who looked even paler than she had outside. "Come and sit, Violet," he said softly, and pulled out the chair opposite from where Dorcas sat, wanting to keep as much distance between them as possible. She cast a wary glance at Daisy and shook her head.

"I - I can't leave her," she said in a voice that was barely above a whisper, then tucked her legs underneath her, settling next to Daisy.

Emmett chastised himself for not thinking that she'd want to stay next to her dog and gave her what he hoped was an encouraging smile. Despite the seriousness of her aunt's accusations, he wanted to hear the rationale behind them before he jumped to conclusions. Her lip trembled and she shifted her gaze back to the dog.

Dorcas opened her mouth, but Emmett gave her a look that had her snap it back shut without a word. His mother set a cup of steaming coffee in front of the woman, and handed another to

Emmett before taking a seat in her usual place, which was perpendicular to Dorcas.

Dorcas lifted the cup, took a cautious sniff and scowled in disgust before she set it back on the table and pushed it away from her, shaking her head. "In the civilized part of the country, we know enough to serve tea to guests."

"Aunt Dorcas, please," Violet pleaded, but her aunt cut her off.

"You're in no position to ask anything of me. You're quite lucky I didn't bring the sheriff of this . . ."

Emmett's eyes widened as his mother slapped the palm of her hand on the table. She used to do the same thing when he and his brothers were younger and would get out of hand.

"Why don't we start at the beginning?" she said. "Emmett, would you please replace Mrs. Montgomery's cup with a clean one and heat some water?"

Emmett clenched his jaw and gave a stiff nod as he rose from the table, forcing himself not to roll his eyes at the request.

"Emmett?" Dorcas's eyebrows lifted and she turned to Violet. "I was told you had married a man named Wyatt."

"Wyatt was my brother," Emmett said stiffly, picking up her cup. "He's deceased."

Dorcas gasped and covered her mouth with her hand and turned to Violet. "Did you poison him as well? You'd probably have gotten away with it too if I hadn't –"

His mother took in a sharp breath and nearly dropped her cup.

"I did no such thing," Violet cried.

Dorcas let out a cold, mirthless laugh. "Sure you didn't. Just like you didn't try to poison your own flesh and blood. Who will believe you didn't do it twice?"

"No more!" Emmett shouted. "You need to leave," he pointed toward the door. Dorcas flinched, almost imperceptibly, but he'd seen it. There was something strange going on here and he was going to find out what it was, but he needed to talk to Violet first.

Dorcas let out a huff and stood. "Very well. Violet, gather your things so we can be on our way before you –"

"No," Emmett turned to Violet. She had her arms wrapped around her waist and tears welled in her eyes as she stared back at him. "Do you want to go with her?" he asked softly.

She pulled her bottom lip between her teeth and shook her head.

He walked to the door and yanked it open, then turned to Violet's aunt. "She is staying. You are leaving," he said coldly. "I'll have Dave take you to the hotel and make arrangements for you to stay there until we can get this sorted out."

Dorcas pressed her lips into a thin line and straightened her spine before walking toward the door. She paused next to Emmett. "Be careful of that one," she warned in a low voice. "She's an accomplished liar and thief. You don't want to end up being her next victim."

Emmett clenched his fists as she flounced past him. "We'll see about that," he muttered and followed her to the buggy to apprise Dave. He readily agreed to take her to the hotel, and within moments the buggy and its occupants were on their way back to Last Chance.

Emmett took a deep breath before going back into the house. Violet had shared very little about her past with him, but even so, nothing could have prepared him for what he'd just witnessed. If what her aunt had said was true, he couldn't have her staying here with his family. Putting them in danger. But if it wasn't? A shiver ran down his spine as he thought about what it must have been like to live with that woman.

He didn't know how, but he was going to figure out what was going on. Emmett pulled the door open and saw his mother kneeling on the floor with her arms wrapped around Violet as she sobbed softly into her shoulder.

He felt a twist in his stomach as he realized there was nothing he wanted more than to be the one holding and comforting her, and he knew, in that moment, that there was no possible way her aunt's accusations could be true.

Emmett closed the door behind him and both his mother and Violet looked up at him. Violet's eyes were red rimmed and puffy from crying and he was struck by the immeasurable sorrow in her expression.

"It's . . . it's not true," Violet said through her sobs. "What she said. I didn't -" she broke off and buried her face back in his mother's shoulder.

His mother patted her back. "Of course you didn't," she murmured, and then looked at Emmett, her face a mixture of anger and concern. "A nastier woman never drew breath," she said, her voice laced with irritation.

"I'm so sorry." Violet lifted her head and sniffed. She pulled away from his mother and placed a hand across Daisy's still form, and wiped the tears off her face with the other. "I knew," she said, staring at her dog, her breath hitching as she spoke. "He - he said she might be coming, but I didn't - I didn't want to believe it. I didn't mean to involve you." Fresh tears streamed down her face. "I - I should have left."

Emmett tried to make sense out of her words, then it dawned on him. The telegram. Whoever the telegram was from had warned her that her aunt was coming.

"Who was the telegram from, Violet?" he asked.

"My attorney in Charleston, Mr. Vesprey."

Before he could ask anything else, the door flew open and Eli burst into the room followed by a tall, lean man with blond hair.

"This is Dr. Spaulding," Eli said, frowning as he took in the scene before him. "Are we too late?"

"No," Emmett said, and nodded a greeting to the doctor, who was already halfway across the room. Dr. Spaulding gave a curt nod back and knelt next to Violet. He placed his black bag next to him and deftly began to examine Daisy.

"I've never seen this type of dog," he remarked as his fingers palpated the dog's legs. "Where did she come from?"

"She was a gift from my father," Violet sniffed. "I believe he got her on the island of Malta. Is she . . . will she . . ." she broke off, covering her mouth with her hand.

"I don't believe she has any internal injuries," he said, moving his examination to Daisy's head.

Emmett watched with great interest as the doctor pried the small animal's eyes open and then her mouth, even going so far as to stick his finger inside. He removed a pair of shears from his black bag, and Violet gasped as he held up a shock of fur next to one of Daisy's ears and prepared to lop it off.

"Must you cut it?"

Dr. Spaulding gave her a cursory glance. "Yes, I need to be able to see what I am looking at," he said, and squeezed the scissors shut. He removed hair in several other spots before returning the scissors to his bag and straightening his back. He ran a hand through his hair and his gaze darted back and forth between Violet and Emmett's mother.

"There doesn't appear to be anything broken, but there are a number of contusions," he said. Seeing Violet's frown, the doctor continued. "A contusion is a bruise. Have you got any sugar?"

It was Emmett's turn to frown now as his mother answered in the affirmative.

"Please, if you would bring it to me, along with some water," the doctor requested.

"I'll get it." Eli rushed to gather the necessary items. Meanwhile, the doctor rummaged through his bag and pulled out a glass dropper.

Dr. Spaulding mixed a small handful of sugar into the cup of water then, using the dropper, carefully dispensed some of the liquid into Daisy's mouth. He did this several more times and they watched in quiet awe as the small dog's nose began to twitch. The next time he brought the dropper to her mouth, her little pink tongue emerged. Seconds later, her dark eyes fluttered open and she let out a small whine as she struggled to sit up.

Emmett breathed a sigh of relief as Violet gathered the dog into her arms and held her close. They thanked Dr. Spaulding, who said he was quite sure Daisy would be just fine, and left them with instructions to bring her back to see him if anything changed.

"Eli, why don't you walk the doctor out and see if there is anything in the barn you can do for a bit while we talk," Emmett said.

Eli glanced at their mother, then nodded without comment and left with the doctor.

"Well, after all that, I think we should sit and finish our coffee," Emmett's mother said, pausing to give Daisy's head a little scratch. She gave Violet an apologetic smile. "I'm happy to hear that she will be fine. I'm sorry she got outside, I didn't even see her run past me."

"It's not your fault, truly. The important thing is she is all right," Violet said, returning her smile and pressing a kiss on the top of Daisy's head.

Emmett arched an eyebrow as he took in Violet's disheveled appearance. Her normally beautiful dark hair was a tangled mess. There were dirt streaks on her face and neck as well as on her gown. An expression of relief softened her tear-stained face, while a hint of fear lingered in her dark eyes. Emmett suddenly found himself wondering absurd things, like what she'd look like holding a child . . . their child.

He gave himself a mental shake to clear his mind of those thoughts and images and turned to the table where his mother stood watching him with a knowing eye. He recalled the words she'd said when they'd spoken a few days earlier: *It doesn't always take a long courtship to fall in love with someone*, and slid a glance back to Violet. *Could it be?*

Mr. Hanna's last telegram played through his mind then, and Emmett's thoughts raced as he considered his possibilities. *None of it would matter if Violet was gone.* He needed to find out what was behind her aunt's preposterous accusations.

Emmett pulled out a chair and waited until Violet was settled before taking the seat across from her. He wanted to be able to see her face while she told her story. Mr. Hanna had told him once that the eyes were the window to the soul, and you could learn a lot about a person by watching their eyes while they spoke. That piece of advice had been particularly useful to him at the bank when making a determination of whether or not to grant a loan.

Emmett's mother refilled their cups and they settled at the table. Violet's gaze darted between him and his mother, then settled on Emmett.

"What my aunt said, it's not the truth," she said.

There was uncertainty coupled with a hint of worry and a deep vulnerability in her eyes. Emmett instinctively knew she wouldn't lie to him.

"I believe you," he said. "Tell us what happened."

She gave him a grateful smile and he felt his heart tug.

"When I became of age," she said, "my father's attorney, Mr. Vesprey, contacted me to discuss the transfer of Father's estate. Aunt Dorcas had control of a part of it up until that point, to ensure I was provided for. As we went through the ledgers I noticed some discrepancies in the expenses my aunt had claimed against the estate."

Emmett lifted his brows and frowned. "What kind of discrepancies?"

Violet shrugged. "There were claims for wardrobes I hadn't procured. Parties and balls we hadn't hosted. But the worst was when Mr. Vesprey told me that Aunt Dorcas had sold Mother and Father's home." She paused and stared into the distance for a moment. Emmett noticed a flicker of pain cross her features before she continued. "I'd planned to live there, get away from my aunt, once I was old enough, but it was gone."

"Oh, goodness. That must have been such a shock," Emmett's mother exclaimed.

Violet nodded. "Yes, it was. Mr. Vesprey said the funds from the sale of the home belonged to Father's estate, but he'd been unsuccessful in collecting them from my aunt."

"So she'd been embezzling?"

Violet pressed her lips together and nodded. "He'd been trying to build a case against her, but it was difficult while I was still under her care because she claimed the funds were being used to provide for me."

"But once you became of age?" his mother asked.

"Because she sold my family home, I had no choice but to continue to stay with her, but she was no longer in control and she didn't like it. I confronted her about the missing funds, and she told me there was no way to prove anything. She said she would see to it that she got what she had coming to her."

Emmett got a sick feeling in his stomach upon hearing that and leaned forward in his chair. "What did she mean by that?"

"She was very upset that all of her access to the funds from the estate were cut off from her. She thought because she was my father's sister that she should have been his heir."

Emmett frowned. He'd worked at the bank long enough to know that wasn't how most estates were distributed.

"But Father made sure her home was paid for and that she would be given a generous stipend each month for the remainder of her days, but she wasn't happy with that. Shortly after that, Mr. Vesprey came to visit and advised me that Aunt Dorcas had inquired about the status of the estate if something should happen to me. He was concerned she might try to do something to me, and advised me to leave by any means possible."

"So you answered Wyatt's advertisement," Emmett said as understanding dawned.

"Yes, it was the only thing I could think of," she said, and turned to look at his mother with a sheepish expression. "My best friend, Annabelle, came up with the idea."

Emmett's mother reached over and placed a reassuring hand on Violet's arm. "Sweet girl, we've discussed this. God brought you to us because you needed us," her gaze flitted to Emmett and back, "however that might be. How were you able to leave?"

Violet's gaze dropped to the cup in front of her as a blush crept up her cheeks. "I didn't tell her I was leaving," she said. She chewed her bottom lip for a second, then continued. "Annabelle and I thought it would be best if I just left. Because of the warning from Mr. Vesprey, we decided Annabelle shouldn't know where I was going either. That way she wouldn't be able to coerce the location from her after I was gone. I haven't been able to even write to Annabelle to let her know I am safe," she said, trying to blink back tears.

"Why has she accused you of attempted murder?" Emmett asked.

"I don't know, really," she said, her gaze not wavering from his. "Shortly before I left Charleston, I became ill. At first I thought I'd just eaten something that had turned, but I grew worse. Aunt Dorcas kept saying the doctor would be by, but he never came. Then I remembered Mr. Vesprey's warning."

Emmett's mother put her hand over her mouth. "You don't think she was behind it, do you?"

Violet nodded. "I do. I had Annabelle bring in some food for me from her house, and refused to eat what Aunt Dorcas served. I recovered almost immediately. When I told my aunt what I suspected she'd done, she said I'd never be able to prove it. That no one would believe me over her. She's very well established and respected in Charleston because of the family name, but I . . . well, I believe her to be . . . unsound.

"I don't believe her intent is to return me to Charleston. She's relying on convincing you that I've done what she's said so she can take me with her, and I believe she intends to kill me once we've left."

Emmett's mother gasped and she looked at Emmett. "We've got to notify Sheriff Darcy," she said.

"There's no proof she's done anything," Violet said, shaking her head in despair. "Mr. Vesprey said they questioned her maid, but found no evidence of foul play. I know I should have told you from the beginning, but after Wyatt . . . everything happened so quickly and then I didn't know what to do," she lowered her gaze, but not before Emmett saw the reflection of tears pooling in her eyes. "I didn't know where else to go."

"You have no need to go anywhere else," his mother said, and rose from her chair to wrap her arms around Violet. "You are family, and you are right where you belong."

Emmett leaned back in his chair while Violet's reality, her incredible raw story of darkness and pain, played through his mind. He glanced at the clock on the mantle. It was nearly half past twelve. If he left immediately, there would still be time.

"I'm going to town," he said.

"But what about dinner?" his mother asked. "Let me cut you a slice of bread."

"There's no time," he said, plucking his hat off the peg and setting it on his head. "Don't hold supper for me. I'll make sure Eli does the chores," he said over his shoulder as he closed the door behind him. He was going to make sure Violet's aunt never bothered her again. One way or another.

Chapter Ten

♥

On the way to town, Emmett mulled over everything Violet had told them and tried to formulate a plan. Violet was right, without proof there was little that could be done . . . legally. Emmett didn't need proof. He believed every word she said unequivocally.

He couldn't imagine what it would be like to have what was supposed to be a trusted family member, the *only* family member you had left, do something so horrific. Emmett admired Violet's intrepidness and her character. Through everything, she managed to figure out how to get away and then, despite not having any idea what she was doing on the farm, never quit trying to be helpful.

The hateful words her aunt had spoken ran through his mind again, and he vowed to make sure Violet never heard them again. Then he thought of something Mr. Hanna had told him early in his banking career. *You mustn't get entangled in matters between family members.*

It was sound advice. But this was different. Wasn't it? He slowed the horse for a moment while he considered why he was making this family matter of Violet's his business. The simple answer was that he wanted to help her. But it was more than that. He wanted her to like him. And, he reasoned, urging the horse to pick up speed, she was family. His family.

As Emmett rode through town toward the Post Office, his attention was drawn to the bank. Something his mother had said niggled in the back of his mind. It was the day Violet made the hard as rock biscuits and spilled a cup of water on his lap. She'd said *thank you for the extra help*. He'd been sending a small amount of money home each month since he'd gotten his job at City National Bank in Denver, but wasn't sure what she meant by *extra* help.

He decided to make a quick stop at the bank and make sure nothing was amiss with his mother's account, and see if there was any other unusual activity that the banker might share with him. Violet's aunt had also accused her of theft, and while Violet hadn't specifically addressed that accusation, and Emmett was sure it was just another preposterous claim, it wouldn't hurt to see if he could invalidate it.

He tied the horse to the post in front of the bank and straightened his hat before walking in. His gaze wandered through the room, taking in the single dark walnut teller counter with its three-sided teller cage comprised largely of crimped wire and channel iron. The exchange window was surrounded by an elaborately designed cast iron plaque and there were two chairs along the wall to the left of the counter. Dust and dirt collected across the top and along the bottom of the counter, as well as in the corners of the room, and the faint odor of pipe tobacco permeated the air.

Through the teller cage, Emmett watched as a short, slight man with disheveled dark hair and thick, bushy side-whiskers rose from behind a large desk littered with papers and approached the counter. Emmett was glad Mr. Hanna wasn't here to see the disarray. He'd always stressed the importance of perception and attention to detail in order to build trust in relationships, including his requirement of staff to be well-groomed at all times. He would be appalled at the state of disrepair the bank was in.

"Can I help you," the man asked, adjusting his eyeglasses, a harried expression on his lean features.

"Good afternoon, I'm Emmett Stapleton. I'd like to-"

"Oh, Mr. Stapleton!" The man's eyebrows shot up. "I'd been hoping you'd come by." He turned and rushed to the gate, opened it and came around to the front of the counter. "My name is Abe Froman," he said, and offered Emmett a timid handshake, his eyes flitted around the room as though he was looking for something. "Your mother made mention that you work at a very prestigious bank in Denver."

Emmett's father had always told his sons *if they don't have a firm handshake or look you in the eye, don't trust them*. He recalled the very firm handshake Mr. Porter, the former bank manager, had had. Emmett had been saddened to learn Mr. Porter had been part of the hunting party that perished in the blizzard the previous fall. Emmett knew him to be meticulous and detailed, and doubted he'd allow the bank to function in its current state.

"Mr. Froman," Emmett said, shaking the man's hand. "I was hoping to speak to the manager." He glanced around the room, but saw no one else. "Is that you?"

Mr. Froman glanced over his shoulder as though he hoped someone would be there, then let out a sigh. "Yes," he said, then quickly amended. "I'm acting manager, that is. Is there something I can help you with?"

"Yes," Emmett said. "As you know, I've been making regular transfers into my mother's account."

"Yes, of course," Mr. Froman said, then frowned. "Is there a problem?"

"No, at least I hope not. Has there been any unusual activity with her account?"

Mr. Froman pushed his glasses up on his nose again and plucked at his mustache with his fingers while he thought. "No," he finally said, shaking his head. "Just your deposits, and those from the younger Mrs. Stapleton."

The younger Mrs. Stapleton? "Violet?"

"Yes," Mr. Froman's face showed just a hint of a smile, then he adjusted his glasses again and continued. "After the unfortunate events of last fall, she came in and asked if I would please make a monthly transaction from her account to your mother's. She was concerned with your brother being gone . . ." He trailed off and gave a sheepish shrug. "She asked me not to say anything. She knew your mother wouldn't accept the money, but you're family."

Emmett nodded. "She has an account here then as well?"

"Oh yes, her attorney in Charleston set it up for her," he said, as if impressed.

Emmett smiled, unable to stop the grin that formed on his lips. Violet's resilience and tenacity continued to impress him. She was so unlike any other woman he'd ever met.

"Are you planning to stay in Last Chance?" Mr. Froman asked, snapping Emmett out of his musings.

"I'm expected back in Denver in short order," Emmett replied, but his voice sounded almost mechanical and without conviction.

Mr. Froman's shoulders drooped and he rubbed the back of his neck. "I see. I'm sorry to hear that. I mean, I'm . . ." He stammered, and a flush of red crept up his face. "Of course you'll be returning to Denver." He pressed his lips into a thin line and nodded his head.

Emmett frowned at his strange comment. "Sorry? Why is that?"

Mr. Froman looked around the room and then settled his gaze on Emmett. "Well, I . . . it's just that I am merely a teller. When Mr. Porter failed to return from the hunting expedition, I was forced to make the choice of taking over operations or closing the bank," he said, his fingers fidgeting with the cuffs of his shirt. "I was hoping . . . that is, well, it's just that my Mrs. is not well."

"I'm sorry to hear that," Emmett said, trying to follow what Mr. Froman was saying.

"Dr. Barnes is of the opinion that a change in climate would be beneficial for her." He cast his gaze down and let out a small sigh. "The truth of the matter is, she is no longer happy here in Last Chance. Not since the blizzards. She's got family back East, and wants to return."

Emmett nodded. "What about the bank?"

"I've been searching for a suitable replacement for myself, but have not had any luck finding someone with banking experience," Mr. Froman said, a wrinkle appearing between his brows. He shifted his weight from one foot to another and pushed his glasses back up his nose. "She's becoming rather," he paused to clear his throat, "impatient, however, and I'm afraid I may have to close the bank. Although I'm not quite sure how to go about that." He muttered that last part under his breath.

Close the bank? Despite the tragedy and huge loss of life that had occurred the previous year, from what Emmett could see, Last Chance was a growing, thriving town. The loss of the bank would have detrimental effects on the town.

"I'd thought, perhaps, with your experience, you might be interested in taking over," Mr. Froman said, tugging on his mustache. "But, of course, your job in Denver awaits."

"Yes, it does," Emmett agreed absently. *Him? Bank manager in Last Chance?* It was something he'd never considered. His life was in Denver. *Or was it?* He'd been so focused on his career that he didn't have many friends. The room he rented was just that, a room. His life consisted of little more than his work at the bank, and how quickly he could advance there.

Emmett had felt so fortunate when Mr. Hanna had taken him under his wing. He'd aspired to be just like him, not like the simple farmer his father was. But Emmett found himself wondering if Mr.

Hanna was happy. Yes, he had fine clothing and was highly respected in the Denver community, but Emmett couldn't recall a single time Mr. Hanna had mentioned a single thing about his life outside of the bank. He'd taught Emmett that the three most important things in life were your career, your reputation, and the balance in your bank account.

He'd listened to Mr. Froman talk about his wife, and the sacrifice he was willing to make for her, and Emmett began to wonder if he was making a mistake. What good was a fancy career and a pile of money in the bank if you had no one to share it with?

His gaze was drawn to the clock that hung on the wall behind Mr. Froman. He needed to stop wool-gathering and focus on the reason he'd come to town in the first place.

"Mr. Froman," Emmett said. "I must be going. Thank you for your time today," he touched the brim of his hat with his fingers and turned to leave.

"Of course," Mr. Froman replied with a ring of disappointment in his voice. "Best of luck to you in Denver, although I do hope you'll consider the offer here."

Emmett paused in the doorway and looked over his shoulder at Mr. Froman. "Thank you, I will," he said, and pulled the door shut behind him.

His next stop was the Sheriff's Office. He explained the situation to Sheriff Darcy, who assured Emmett he'd check with his counterparts in Charleston to see if there were, in fact, any charges pending against Violet. He also said he'd have them run a check on Violet's aunt. Emmett thanked him and made his way back up the street to the Post Office.

A couple emerged from the diner as Emmett walked past, sending the aroma of freshly baked bread and coffee into the air. His stomach grumbled, reminding him that he hadn't eaten dinner yet. He pulled his watch out of his pocket and looked at it. It was nearly two o'clock. Deciding he had the time, Emmett turned and walked into the diner.

"Emmett," a man's voice called to him from the other side of the dining room. He turned his head and saw Amos Gruby seated at a table with several other people. Amos had been a couple years ahead of Emmett in school, but they'd known each other most of their lives. He waved Emmett over.

Amos stood and shook Emmett's hand. "I heard you were in town," he said, and introduced Emmett to the others at the table.

Emmett had met Amos's wife, Lotty, before but didn't know Cullen Parker. He'd married Ruby Fulton, who sat next to him, just that winter, and the other man was Cullen's brother, Ben.

"We just got here," Amos said, sitting back down. "You should join us." He gestured to the empty chair next to him.

"Thank you, I'd appreciate the company," Emmett said, surprised to find he actually meant it.

He couldn't remember the last time he'd dined with friends, besides Violet, that is. As he sat, Emmett thought for a moment, trying to place where he'd heard the name *Ben Parker*. Then he remembered the conversation he'd had with Eli. Emmett had meant to talk with Ben about the possibility of him doing some work out at the farm, but hadn't found the time. This would be the perfect opportunity.

Nearly two hours later, Emmett stepped out of the diner. He'd enjoyed his visit with Amos, and getting to know Cullen and Ben, and he and Ben had worked out an arrangement for Ben to work as a hired hand at his mother's farm. He'd just started walking when he heard someone call his name. He turned and saw Sheriff Darcy lift his arm and wave him over from across the street. Emmett waited for a buckboard to pass, then hurried across the road to where the Sheriff waited for him.

"I've just heard back from my contact in Charleston," the Sheriff said, and he pulled a telegram out of his pocket. "It's just as you thought. They have no information about any criminal charges pending or otherwise against Violet Montgomery, or Violet Stapleton."

Emmett let out a pent up breath. He'd never doubted her, but it was still a relief to hear the words spoken aloud.

"There is, however," the Sheriff continued, "an investigation and new charges have been made against Dorcas Montgomery. You say she's here? In Last Chance?"

Emmett smiled, unable to stop the grin that formed on his lips. "Yes, she's staying at the hotel." His smile faded as he recalled something Violet had said. "Violet believes she may be unsound," he said somberly. "From what I've seen of her, I would agree with that."

Sheriff Darcy nodded. "I'll have my deputy come with me to the hotel to arrest her. We'll hold her here until arrangements can be made to have her transferred back to Charleston. Thank you for bringing this matter to my attention," he extended his hand to Emmett and they shook. "You can assure Mrs. Stapleton that she no longer needs to worry about her aunt."

"Thank you," Emmett said, and watched him walk down the street toward the Sheriff's Office. A wave of relief flooded him and he became anxious to return back to the farm to give Violet the news. He had one more stop to make.

Emmett made his way toward the Post Office and as he walked, he paid closer attention to the buildings and businesses he passed. If what Amos said about the influx of newcomers to town was true, Last Chance needed a fully operational bank. He cogitated about his job in Denver and Mr. Hanna's promise of promotion, then about Mr. Froman's offer here in Last Chance.

He stopped with his hand on the doorknob of the Post Office and looked over his shoulder at the bustling street behind him. It had been nearly six weeks since he'd stepped off the stagecoach at the Depot next door. He'd never intended to stay even half as long as he had. The promotion he'd been promised wouldn't wait for him indefinitely, Emmett knew what he needed to do, and it would be much easier to return to Denver knowing that Violet would be safe.

"Good afternoon, Faith," he said as he walked in. "I need to send a telegram."

"Emmett," she smiled. "It's nice to see you again. Would this be going to Mr. John Hanna again?"

Emmett had sent a couple of telegrams to Mr. Hanna since he'd been in Last Chance to keep him apprised of his situation. This would be the last one. "Yes, that's right," he said, and let out a sigh.

Faith nodded. "What would you like it to say?" She picked up a pencil and held it poised over a sheet of paper while she waited.

He cleared his throat. "Returning to Denver. Will arrive by end of week. Request meeting."

He'd liked to have said more, but telegrams were costly to send and he'd spent more than enough on them since he'd been back in Last Chance.

Faith's gaze snapped to his and a little furrow appeared between her brows. For a second it looked like she was going to say something, but then she turned her attention back to the telegram.

Emmett waited until it had been sent, then paid for the telegram and bid Faith a good day. From the Post Office, he went to the Depot and purchased a ticket for the stagecoach to the train station, and a train ticket to Denver.

The ride back to the farm passed quickly as Emmett made a list in his mind of what he needed to do. For the first time in years, he felt a quiet confidence in what he wanted to do with his life. As he rode into the farmyard, his body and mind relaxed and a strange feeling of peace came over him. A feeling of rightness . . . of home.

"You mean they are arresting her?" Violet stared at him with a mixture of awe and admiration. "But...how?"

Emmett explained about his visit to the Sheriff's Office and the telegram the Sheriff had received. "The Sheriff said she'd be taken back to Charleston soon. He didn't have any other information."

"So she can't..." Violet trailed off.

"No, she can't hurt you or steal from you anymore."

Violet grew still and stared at a spot on the wall behind Emmett for a long moment before her gaze went back to his. "I would be able to return to Charleston then, if I wanted?"

Emmett's stomach dropped and his mouth went dry. He'd never considered the possibility that she'd want to return to Charleston. He opened his mouth to protest, but nothing came out. Violet had come here and married his brother seeking refuge. Now that her aunt was no longer a threat, and her husband was dead, she had no reason to stay. He frowned and looked at his mother, quite sure that she wore the same grim, ashen expression as he.

"Of course you could," his mother said, her voice wavering ever so slightly. "You always have a home here and don't need to make any hasty decisions. Perhaps you will find a reason to stay," she gave Emmett a pointed look.

Emmett frowned and dropped his gaze. He could feel the weight of their stares bearing down on him. He squeezed his eyes shut while he tried to think. He wasn't ready. He was going to have to alter his plan. He wanted to talk to Violet alone, but needed to speak to his mother first.

"I will write to my attorney and seek his advice," Violet finally said.

Before Emmett could respond, the door opened and Eli came in, his clothes and hands dirty from doing chores.

"What's for supper?" he asked.

"I made stew," their mother answered. "Why don't you go wash up? You're a mess."

Seeing Eli reminded Emmett of his dinner with Amos and the Parkers.

"Eli, while I was in town I met the Parkers and asked Ben if he'd be interested in working here as a hired hand, and he agreed. Cullen spoke highly of your skill with wood and thought perhaps you'd be able to spend a little more time helping him at the mill with Ben working here."

Eli's brows shot up and his face broke into a grin. "Really? Can I, Ma?"

Their mother pressed her lips into a thin line. "Emmett, can I have a word with you? In private?"

Eli shot Emmett a smile as Emmett followed his mother outside, feeling like a small child getting ready to be scolded.

Once they were away from the house, she turned and narrowed her eyes at him. "Emmett Stapleton, what are you doing?" she demanded.

"Mother, I have a plan." Emmett tugged his ear and grinned sheepishly. "Remember when you offered me Grandmother's ring and I didn't take it?"

A small gasp escaped his mother's lips and she nodded, her eyes dancing.

He cleared his throat and continued. "You were right, I just couldn't see it. But I do now. I love her, Mother, and I want to ask her to marry me. Can I please have Grandmother's ring?"

Chapter Eleven

♥

V iolet sank into the nearest chair as Emmett's words replayed in her mind. Aunt Dorcas would no longer be able to hurt her. She didn't know whether she should laugh or cry. The fact that her aunt was facing criminal charges for what she'd done to her hurt. Yet at the same time, it brought Violet a measure of relief, as if a great weight had been lifted from her shoulders.

She could go back to Charleston now, if she wanted. The question was, did she want to? There was sure to be scandal when news got out about

Aunt Dorcas's arrest. If she returned, everywhere she went she'd be the subject of gossip. Of pointed fingers and whispering. It wasn't like that here in Last Chance.

"You are exactly where you are meant to be," Cora had told her. *Was it true?* Cora assured her that she had a home here, but surely she couldn't live here indefinitely. Violet glanced around the cozy house. Eli was washing up at the sink and through the window, she could see Emmett and Cora talking outside. When she'd mentioned the possibility of returning to Charleston, Emmett had gotten the strangest look on his face, almost one of panic. Was it possible that he wanted her to stay too?

She didn't want to leave. These people had become her family. She watched through the window as Cora threw her arms around Emmett, and a wide smile lit up his handsome features. Violet's stomach went tight as a realization struck her. She loved Emmett, out of nowhere, pure and simple.

"*God brought you to us for a reason.*"

Cora had seen it before she had. A sudden wave of emotion swept over Violet and she began to cry. She loved him, and he was going back to Denver.

The door opened and Cora and Emmett stepped back inside. Violet turned her head and covered her face with her hands, trying to stop the sobs from escaping, her chest tightening with the effort.

"What happened?" Emmett asked and rushed to her side.

"I don't know," Eli said and gave a helpless shrug. "She was staring out the window and just started to cry."

Violet dropped her chin and the sobs she'd been trying to hold back came pouring out. It was as if a dam broke loose and all the emotions she'd bottled up inside her since her parents died burst forth.

Emmett gathered her into an embrace and felt the shudder of her sobs as she clung to him.

The feel of Emmett's arms around her was something Violet was certain she would never forget. Other than her father, she had never been held by a man. Except for a quick hug before he'd left on the hunting trip, Wyatt had shown her no affection. This was different though. Just being in Emmett's arms was like heaven. It felt like where she belonged and she wished she could stay like this forever.

"Are you all right?" he asked softly.

Emmett's breath was warm against her ear and sent shivers down her spine. Out of the corner of her eye, Violet saw Cora emerge from her bedroom. She was suddenly very aware of Cora and Eli's presence, and embarrassment heated her face. She pulled out of his embrace and swiped at tears on her cheeks.

"I'm sorry," she sputtered, her face growing hotter by the second. She'd been taught that a lady maintained control over her emotions. "I don't know what came over me."

"Are you all right?" Emmett repeated, staring in her eyes.

Violet glanced at Cora, who gave her a tender smile that filled Violet with a warmth that caused fresh tears to well up in her eyes. She slid her gaze back to Emmett and nodded, taking the handkerchief he offered and dabbing her eyes with it.

"You've had a day," Cora said. "I'll make you a cup of tea." She turned to Emmett. "Why don't you take Violet out for a bit of fresh air while I heat the kettle?"

"I'll do it," Eli broke in.

"No," Cora all but shouted. All three of them looked at her in surprise and spots of red blossomed on her cheeks. "Eli, you stay and help me in here," she said, and put her hand on his arm to still him. "Go on, then," she gave Emmett a knowing smile and waved her free hand toward the door. "I'll have the tea hot and ready by the time you come back in."

Cora's eyes were bright and there was an underlying excitement in her voice that sparked Violet's curiosity. She wondered what had transpired between Cora and Emmett while they'd been outside. Her gaze went back and forth between them before she decided she must be imagining things. She was tired and getting a bit of fresh air did sound like a good idea.

Emmett offered her his elbow and Violet gave a hesitant glance to Daisy, who lay sleeping on the pallet Cora had put together.

Cora followed her gaze. "Don't worry about Daisy," she assured her. "I'll watch over her."

Violet gave Cora a grateful smile. Daisy had been sleeping most of the afternoon, but had eaten a little bit and was breathing normally again. "Thank you," she said, and threaded her arm through Emmett's. Cora followed them to the door and gave Emmett's arm a squeeze before shutting the door behind them.

They walked toward the creek in comfortable silence. It was late in the afternoon and the air was filled with the scent of honeysuckle and grass. Birds chirped, singing their last songs of the day before they went to wherever it was that birds went at night, and there was an odd-sounding trill coming from the trees along the creek.

Violet stopped and tilted her head to the side, her brows pulling together. "What is that strange noise?"

Emmett looked in the direction of the trees and was quiet for a moment while he listened. He turned to Violet, and when he smiled at her, the corners of his eyes crinkled.

"The cicadas make that sound. Don't you have them in Charleston?"

"I don't believe so." Violet frowned. "I can't recall hearing that before."

"You'd remember," Emmett chuckled. "They get quite loud at night. They are just now coming out of the ground."

"They don't bite, do they?" she asked, her eyes wide. Violet had a strong dislike of insects and had seen more varieties of them in her short time on the farm than she had her entire life in Charleston.

Emmett gave her arm a light squeeze. "No, you are perfectly safe and in fact, will likely never see one. They tend to stay in the trees."

"Then I shall avoid any activities involving trees," she said with a smirk. Emmett laughed and she joined him and they resumed walking.

It felt nice walking beside Emmett. Safe. Comfortable. Violet didn't know how much longer Emmett had planned to stay in Last Chance, but she was sure that she didn't want him to go. She glanced at him out of the corner of her eye. How exactly did one go about telling someone you loved them? What if he didn't reciprocate?

They stopped near a fallen tree along the slope to the valley below. The sun cast long shadows across the creek and a light breeze ruffled the leaves in the trees. Emmett released Violet's arm and ran a hand through his hair.

"Violet," he said, then cleared his throat and ran his hands down the front of his trousers. "There's something I need to tell you."

Violet's stomach tightened and her mouth went dry. He was going to tell her he was leaving, going back to Denver. She didn't know why she thought he'd stay. Would he still go if he knew how she felt?

"I've got to return to Denver . . ."

Violet squeezed her eyes shut not wanting to hear any more. Her heart thumped wildly in her chest and her fingers tingled. Could she risk telling him? Could she risk not telling him?

"I love you." The words tumbled from her lips before she could stop them. Had she really said it aloud? Emmett's eyes widened, confirming she had indeed uttered the words. Her cheeks flamed.

"What?" He blinked at her as if he too wasn't sure she'd actually said what she had.

"I . . . I love you," she whispered. She lowered her gaze and held her breath while she waited for him to speak. Would he mock her? Would he despise her? Was there any possibility he might . . . No, she couldn't allow herself to think it.

Emmett placed a finger under her chin and slowly lifted her head. Violet trembled as she raised her eyes to meet his. His eyes held neither judgment or reproach, but rather a wonder and warmth that made Violet's breath catch.

"I love you too." His mouth curved with tenderness.

"You do? But . . . but you just said you were going back to Denver."

"You didn't let me finish," he said, amusement dancing in his eyes.

"Finish," Violet said, and a warmth spread through her chest as she stared at him and waited.

"I'm going back to Denver to meet with Mr. Hanna, and settle my affairs there so I can take over as bank manager here in Last Chance. When I come back . . ." Emmett paused and pulled a small leather box out of the pocket of his frock coat. He stepped back and dropped to one knee. "I want to marry you, if you'll have me."

He opened the box, revealing a beautiful ornate gold band. In the center lay a large amethyst surrounded by small pearls. Violet's breath caught in her throat as he reached for her hand.

"Violet Montgomery Stapleton, will you do me the honor of becoming my wife?"

Her eyes widened, then misted, and her lips began to quiver. "Yes," she cried. "Yes, I will."

Emmett rose, leaned in and softly pressed his lips against hers. Tentative at first, their kiss was barely more than a breath against each other's lips but quickly grew more intense, sending Violet's stomach plummeting.

He gently pulled away, and she clung to his arms to steady herself.

He kissed the tip of her nose. "Let's go tell Mother," he said, smiling down at her.

Cora had been right, Violet realized. God had put her right where she needed to be. She nodded as she gazed into his eyes. In them she saw love and the promise of a future she never dreamed was possible.

Keep reading for a sneak peek at Laura's other Blizzard Bride book, A Groom for Ruby.

Leave a Review

♥

Did you enjoy this book? Please considering leaving a review! They can be as long or short as you want and are very much appreciated. Thank you!

♥

November, 1878 - Last Chance, Nebraska

Ruby Fulton slowly stirred the small pot of oatmeal with one hand and pulled her threadbare shawl tighter around her shoulders with the other. She could hear the wind howling outside and the heat from the cook stove brought little comfort to the drafty house. It would only get colder as winter approached. Ruby's shoulders slumped as she thought about everything that needed to be done. Cyrus hadn't gotten around to taking care of any of the winter chores before he'd left with the hunting group that never returned.

Ruby shuddered thinking about it. The men had only been gone for a couple of days when the temperature suddenly plummeted. Thunder and lightning filled the skies and seemingly out of nowhere, a blizzard began to rage. The snow and wind continued for two days straight, dropping nearly four feet of snow on the ground. Ruby managed to save her flock of chickens by bringing them into the house with her, something she'd never dare to do if Cyrus had been home. Once the snow stopped, she frantically cleaned the mess they'd made in the small house. It wasn't until Sheriff Applebee stopped by the farm a couple of days later that she heard how many people perished in the blizzard.

With no sign of Cyrus and eggs piling up, she finally decided to make a trip into town. Mr. Talley at the mercantile regularly bought eggs from them, but Cyrus usually insisted on taking them to town by himself. He allowed her to go with him to church once a month, but said that any more than that wasn't necessary. Ruby suspected it had more to do with his proclivity to sleep in than anything.

While in town, she'd heard talk about the missing hunting party, but Pastor Collins had convinced the townsfolk to wait a few more days for them to make their way home before sending out a search party. Heather Barnes, the butcher's wife, was handing out smoked meat and Ruby gratefully took a sack. Cyrus hadn't done any hunting that fall, and their food store for the winter was far less than they'd need. While she'd gotten resourceful at making what little food they had stretch, she was more concerned than ever about how they'd make it through another harsh Nebraska winter.

When she returned home from town that day, she prayed fervently that Cyrus would not return from the hunting trip. Ruby had come to Last Chance five years earlier as a mail order bride, much like many of the other women in town. She'd been abandoned as a young child, and only had vague recollections of someone that may or may not have been her mother. Somehow, she'd ended up in an orphanage in St. Louis, although she wasn't sure if that was where she was born. It was at the suggestion of one of the nuns there that she answered Cyrus's advertisement.

Ruby had high hopes of improving her station in life, but quickly learned that life with Cyrus Fulton was no improvement. He was a lazy man, and after several years had passed and she produced no heir for him, he became violent. She'd become adept at hiding or explaining most of the bruises over the years, but the pity she saw reflected in the eyes of the women in town shamed her to her core.

Not quite two weeks later, the second blizzard struck. This one came during the night. Ruby heard the wind pick up with the same eerie sound as it had when the first blizzard came. Again, she ran to the barn and brought her flock of chickens into the house. So many people lost livestock during the first storm, she knew she'd be able to sell her eggs and perhaps buy some dry goods with the money before Cyrus came back. She didn't know what he did with the egg money, but suspected it was spent at the saloon in town.

Once that storm passed and she'd managed a second trip into town, she learned that not only had all of the men in the hunting party been killed, but the group of men that had gone to retrieve their bodies had likely died too. Mrs. Talley told her that Pastor Collins preached that God was angry and was punishing the town. Ruby was overcome with guilt. This was her fault. God was angry with her. She had prayed Cyrus wouldn't return and as a result, none of the men would return. The oatmeal blurred as tears filled her eyes.

"I'm hungry, Miss Ruby," a small voice interrupted Ruby's thoughts.

She hastily wiped her cheeks and turned to face the young boy, who looked back at her with earnest eyes. "It's almost ready, Everett. Have you washed your hands?"

"Yes, Miss Ruby."

"All right then, why don't you set the table and by the time you're done, this will be ready."

He nodded and quietly did as she bid. The boy was always hungry, although by looking at his small frame, you'd never know it. Gideon and Ida Henzel owned the property adjacent to hers, and Everett was their young son. Gideon ran the sawmill, which was located on the large creek that ran through his property. They were an older couple, and while Ruby didn't know much about them, she had gleaned through bits and pieces of what Cyrus told her that Everett had been an unexpectedly late addition to their family. His birth had been quite difficult and Ida never fully recovered. Gideon blamed the child, and Ruby suspected the six years Everett had been alive had not been easy ones for him.

Gideon had gone with the hunting party, and Ruby would never forget the haunted look on the little boy's face when he showed up at her door a couple of days after the second blizzard asking her to help him wake his momma. She'd ran with him the half mile back to their farm, but it was too late. Mrs. Henzel was gone. Ruby wasn't sure what had happened, but suspected when Ida had learned Gideon wasn't coming back, she had simply given up.

She'd bundled Everett up in clothing she found in the Henzel's house and walked with him to town to see Mr. Blanchard, the undertaker. Mr. Blanchard had dark circles under his eyes and looked completely overwhelmed. When she told him about Mrs. Henzel and asked what she should do with Everett, he told her to leave him at the diner. Hollie Dawson was taking in some of the orphans, and perhaps would have room for him, unless of course, she wanted to take him in herself. He wasn't aware of any family the Henzel's had in the area, but perhaps Pastor Collins, or Faith, who was now operating the post office, would know more.

Ruby had looked down at Everett's sad little face and her heart wrenched. She would provide a home for the little boy as long as he needed one. Vowing to have a conversation with Faith next time she came to town, they made a quick stop at the mercantile where Mrs. Talley gave Everett two gumdrops, and Ruby bought a bit of sugar with some of her egg money. She could tell Mrs. Talley wanted to ask her about the child, but was grateful when she didn't. She wasn't used to being in town and felt intimidated by most of the townsfolk.

They stopped back at the Henzel's on their way home from town that day. Ruby collected the one horse and cow that hadn't perished in the blizzard, along with the few articles of clothing Everett had, and the unlikely foursome made their way home. While Ruby managed to save her chickens, the small amount of livestock they owned perished in the blizzards. She had gratefully accepted responsibility of the Henzel's horse and cow until someone came along to claim Everett.

Ruby pushed the memories aside and pulled the pot off the stove. She scooped the steaming oatmeal into the bowls Everett had set on the table. Everett stared at the bowl with a longing in his eyes, but he made no move to pick up his spoon. Ruby knew he was waiting for her to let him know it was okay for him to eat it, and she was filled with a profound sadness for the little boy. On a whim, she reached into the small cabinet next to the dry sink and pulled out a small bag of sugar and the dish of butter. She watched Everett's eyes grow large as she placed a small pat of butter and a little sprinkle of sugar on his oatmeal.

"Go ahead and eat, Everett, before it gets cold," she smiled at the boy.

Everett picked up his spoon and a hint of a smile crossed his lips. "Thank you, Miss Ruby."

Ruby's heart swelled. It was the first time she'd seen anything that resembled a smile on his small face since he'd come to stay with her. She sat across from him and ate her plain oatmeal, letting it fill her with its warmth. The wind continued to howl outside, making the blankets she had tacked over the windows flap slightly and every now and then a little puff of snow would come through the walls where the chinking needed repair. Another thing Cyrus hadn't gotten around to before he'd left on the hunting trip. Ruby thought about all the work that needed to be done before the coldest part of winter came and set her spoon on the table. She was no longer hungry. Everett had just spooned the last of his oatmeal into his mouth and she pushed her bowl towards him.

"Can you do me a favor and finish mine?" she asked. "I'm plum filled up."

The boy nodded and pulled her bowl in front of him, eagerly digging his spoon into what remained of her breakfast, while Ruby tried to figure out what she was going to do. Mrs. Talley told her about the ad the women from town placed, looking for grooms to come to town, mostly at Pastor Collins' insistence. The last thing she wanted was another husband, but she knew she couldn't manage all of the repairs on her own and she didn't have anywhere else to go. She closed her eyes and rubbed her forehead. She got herself into this situation, it would be up to her to get herself back out.

"Miss Ruby, are you feeling poorly?"

Ruby opened her eyes and met Everett's concerned gaze. "No, Everett, I'm fine. Why do you ask?"

"Momma would close her eyes and rub her head just like that, and then she'd have to lay down for a long time. Only last time, she didn't get back up."

Ruby felt the back of her throat grow tight as Everett's pale brown eyes filled with tears. She walked around the table and pulled him into her arms, but released him when she felt him stiffen. He wiped his eyes with his small fists and the sorrow she'd seen on his face was quickly replaced with the blank expression he usually wore. She had always wanted a family, with lots of noisy children, but was relieved when she was unable to get pregnant with Cyrus's child. She didn't want to bring a child into their home to suffer at his heavy hand. But now, having Everett to care for, Ruby realized she didn't know the first thing about raising children and felt horribly inadequate. What should she do, for example, when Everett woke in the night, screaming in terror? She had no idea, but she resolved to be patient with him and let him come to her on his own time.

She watched as a shiver ran through Everett's slim shoulders. In an effort to make the rapidly dwindling woodpile last longer, Ruby had been putting a minimal amount of wood in the cook stove. But knew she'd need to come up with a solution.

Ruby quickly did their dishes and added one more small piece of wood to the fire. Everett had moved to the pallet she'd made for him on the floor next to the cook stove and huddled under his blanket. She'd given him the nice thick quilt she'd been gifted by Altar Pennington when she moved to Last Chance. Cyrus hadn't wanted her to accept it, saying they didn't need charity, but Ruby took it anyway. That was before she understood the cost of defying his wishes. It had become her most precious possession, reminding her that even in the worst situation there was kindness and beauty in the world.

She stared at the colorful pattern on the quilt for a moment, when an idea came to her. "Everett, bundle up, we're going to town."

Get a free book! Sign up for Laura's newsletter and get Snowflakes & Second Chances, a subscriber exclusive novella, for free!

About Laura

Laura Ashwood is a USA Today Bestselling author of sweet contemporary and historical western romance, and women's fiction.

In her novels, Laura brings to life characters and relationships that will warm your heart and fill you with hope. Her stories often have themes involving redemption, forgiveness, and family.

Laura and her husband live in northeast Minnesota, which is the setting for many of her stories. She has a full time day job as an executive administrative assistant, and in her spare time, she likes to read, cook and spend time with her husband. She is a devoted grandmother and chihuahua lover.

She is a member of American Christian Fiction Writers (ACFW) and Women's Fiction Writers of America (WFWA).

Find her on Facebook, Bookbub, Instagram, Pinterest, Twitter, and Goodreads. Go to www.lauraashwood.com to see all her books.

If you liked this book, please take a minute to leave a review for it. Authors (Laura included) really appreciate this, and it helps draw more readers to books they might like. Thank you!